*Should Jo seriously consider Hugh's request? Could she go to London and help Hugh with little Ivy for just two short weeks?*

The offer was very tempting. If she tried to balance the pros and cons, there were so many pros.... Two weeks in London...doing a good deed for Ivy's sake....

What about the cons? There had to be reasons why she shouldn't go.

Hugh.

Hugh and his gorgeousness. Two weeks with him and she'd be head over heels in love with the man. Even though he would remain polite and charming, she would fall all the way in love, and she'd come home an emotional wreck.

**Barbara Hannay** was born in Sydney, educated in Brisbane and has spent most of her adult life living in tropical North Queensland, where she and her husband have raised four children. While she has enjoyed many happy times camping and canoeing in the bush, she also delights in an urban lifestyle—chamber music, contemporary dance, movies and dining out. An English teacher, she has always loved writing, and now, by having her stories published, she is living her most cherished fantasy. Visit her Web site at www.barbarahannay.com

## Books by Barbara Hannay

HARLEQUIN ROMANCE®
3841—THE CATTLEMAN'S ENGLISH ROSE*
3845—THE BLIND DATE SURPRISE*
3849—THE MIRRABROOK MARRIAGE*

*Southern Cross Ranch trilogy

# CHRISTMAS GIFT: A FAMILY

## Barbara Hannay

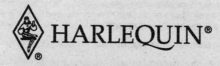

HARLEQUIN®

TORONTO • NEW YORK • LONDON
AMSTERDAM • PARIS • SYDNEY • HAMBURG
STOCKHOLM • ATHENS • TOKYO • MILAN • MADRID
PRAGUE • WARSAW • BUDAPEST • AUCKLAND

ISBN 0-373-03873-9

CHRISTMAS GIFT: A FAMILY

First North American Publication 2005.

# CHAPTER ONE

CHRISTMAS EVE. Oh, joy! For Jo Berry it meant sitting behind a shop counter in Bindi Creek, staring out through the dusty front window at the heat haze shimmering on the almost empty main street, and trying not to think about all the fabulous parties she was missing back in the city.

She was especially trying not to think about the office party tonight. Mind you, she had a feeling things might get out of hand. Her friend, Renee, was determined to nail a big career boost by impressing the boss but, apart from buying something clingy and skimpy to wear, her idea of pitching for a promotion usually involved clearing her desk of sharp objects.

Jo still clung to the belief that a girl could smash her way through the glass ceiling via non-stop slog and professionalism, without the aid of deep cleavage, or tying the boss up with tinsel.

Still, she would have liked to be in Brisbane tonight. She enjoyed her friends' company and it was great fun to be on the fringes of an occasional outrageous party.

It wasn't her friends' wild antics that had stopped her from partying in the city. Every Christmas she took her annual leave and travelled home to help out in her family's shop.

And no, she wasn't a goody two-shoes, but honestly, what else could a girl do when she had a dad on an invalid pension and a mum who was run off her feet trying to play Santa Claus to half a dozen children while preparing Christmas dinner, *plus* running Bindi Creek's only general store during the pre-Christmas rush?

Not that anyone actually rushed in Bindi Creek.

At least…no one usually rushed.

Nothing exciting happened.

And yet…right now there was someone in a very great hurry.

From her perch on a stool behind the counter, Jo watched with interest as a black four-wheel drive scorched down the street, screeched to an abrupt and noisy halt in the middle of the road and then veered sharply to park on the wrong side of the road—directly outside the shop.

A lanky dark-haired stranger jumped out.

A very handsome, lanky dark-haired stranger.

*Oh, wow!*

He was quite possibly the most gorgeous man Jo had ever seen, not counting movie stars, Olympic athletes or European princes in her favourite celebrity magazines.

In spite of the layer of dust that covered his vehicle and the intense, sweltering December heat, he was dressed in city clothes—tailored camel-coloured trousers and a white business shirt, although as a concession to the heat his shirt was open at the neck and his long sleeves were rolled back to his elbows to reveal lightly tanned, muscular forearms.

Jo slid from her stool and tucked a wing of brown hair behind one ear as she stood waiting for the ping of the bell over the shop door. *Please, please come in, you gorgeous thing.*

But the newcomer lingered on the footpath, studying her mum's window display.

Jo couldn't help staring at him.

As he stood with his wide shoulders relaxed and his hands resting lightly on his lean hips, she decided there was a certain elegant charm in the way his soft dark hair had been ruffled and messed into spikes. And there was definite appeal in the very masculine way he rubbed his lightly stubbled jaw as he studied her mother's dreadful tinsel-draped arrangement of tinned plum puddings, boxes of shortbread and packets of chocolate-covered sultanas.

He lifted his gaze and peered inside the shop and, before Jo could duck, his eyes—light blue or green, she couldn't be sure—met hers. Darn, he'd caught her staring.

She felt her cheeks grow hot as he stared back. Then he smiled. But it was rather a stiff smile and she sensed instantly that he was searching for something. By the time he entered the shop her curiosity was fully aroused.

'Good afternoon,' she said warmly. He was close

enough now for her to see that his eyes were green rather than blue and fringed by the blackest of lashes. 'Can I help you?'

This time his smile was of the slightly crooked variety, the kind that should come with a health warning about dangers to women.

'I'll just look around for a moment,' he said, casting a doubtful glance at the bags of sugar and flour and the shelves of tinned food that filled the store.

As soon as he spoke Jo realised he was English. His voice was deep and rich—refined and mellow—reminding her of actors in Jane Austen movies and men who lived in stately homes surrounded by green acres of parkland and edged by forest.

'Look around as much as you like,' she said, trying to sound casual, as if divine Englishmen were a regular part of life in Bindi Creek. And then, because he wasn't a local, she added, 'Just sing out if I can be of any help.'

At times like this, when the shop wasn't busy, she usually amused herself by trying to guess what a customer might buy. What was this guy after? Engine oil? Shaving cream? *Condoms?*

From the far side of the shop he called, 'Do you have any dolls? Perhaps a baby doll?'

*Good grief.*

'I want the best possible gift for a little girl.' It was a command rather than a request. 'Little girls still play with dolls, don't they?'

'Some of them do. But I'm sorry, we don't have any dolls here.'

He frowned. 'You must have little tea sets? Or perhaps a music box?'

In a general store in the middle of the outback? Where did he think he was? A toy shop? 'Sorry, we don't have anything like that.'

'Nothing suitable at all?'

*Think, Jo, think…* She walked towards him along the aisles, checking the shelves as critically as he had. Food, household items and pet supplies, a few basic hardware products, a tiny collection of paperback novels… 'I assume you're looking for a Christmas present?'

'Yes, for a little girl. She's five years old.'

It was the same age as her little sister, Tilly. Jo shook her head. 'I'm afraid you're not going to have much luck here.'

She pointed to the old-fashioned glass jars on the counter. 'We have some fancy sweets and chocolates especially for Christmas.'

'I guess they might do.' He groaned and ran long fingers through his ruffled hair. Jo caught the glint of gold.

'I'd better get something as a fallback.' He began to pick up items at random—throw-away pens, Christmas decorations, a wooden ruler and a school notebook.

Thinking of the beautiful baby doll with a complete change of clothes that she'd bought in Brisbane for Tilly, Jo decided he definitely needed help. But given their limited stock it wasn't going to be easy.

How intriguing… What was this man doing out here in the middle of nowhere?

'How far are you travelling?' she asked.

'To Agate Downs.'

'Oh, I know that property. The Martens' place. It's not far. So you're looking for a present for the little girl they're caring for, are you?'

He looked startled. 'You know her?' He moved closer, his expression more intense.

'Ivy? This is a small town. Sure, I've met her. Do you know what she likes?'

His throat worked. 'No, I've never met her.'

'She's a lovely little thing.' Jo was being totally honest. She'd been quite smitten by the little girl. She had the most exquisite face Jo had ever seen on a child and her prettiness was all the more striking because it contrasted so strongly with the ugly scars on her arm. The poor little mite had been terribly burned in an accident a few years ago. 'Ivy's been in here to shop with Ellen Marten a couple of times this week.'

'Really?'

The eagerness in his voice and his eyes was perplexing. Jo looked at him sharply. Was she getting carried away or was there a resemblance between this man and the child? Ivy's hair was dark and her eyes were clear green like his.

What was going on? Could he be Ivy's father? Jo

didn't like to be too nosy, so she hadn't asked the Martens about Ivy's parents, but she'd heard rumours about a tragedy and there'd actually been talk about an estranged father coming to claim her.

Her customer sighed and gave a little shake of his head. 'I'd completely forgotten that a little girl at Christmas needs a present.'

She felt a rush of sympathy. *Come on, Jo, do something to help.*

'Would you like some of these?' she asked, lifting the lid on a huge jar of chocolates wrapped in red, silver and gold foil. 'Ivy's quite partial to them.' Just yesterday she'd slipped the little girl a chocolate when Ellen Marten wasn't looking and she'd been rewarded by a beaming smile.

'I'll take the lot,' he said, looking exceptionally pleased. 'And I'll have a couple of tins of the short-bread and a bag of those nuts.'

Jo lifted the metal scoop and said, 'Perhaps I could gift wrap these things to make them look a little more festive?'

She was rewarded by another of his dangerous smiles. 'That would be wonderful.'

Leaning one hip against the counter, he folded his arms across his chest and watched her as she began to wrap his purchases in red sparkly paper. She felt self-conscious as his green eyes watched her hands at work, cutting and folding paper, reaching for sticky tape and then measuring lengths of shiny silver and gold ribbon.

If it had been any other customer she would have chattered away, but she was too absorbed by the mystery of his connection with Ivy.

He didn't seem in a hurry so she took her time making the gifts as pretty as she could, adding a sprinkle of glitter and a tiny white fluffy snowman on the chocolates.

'Thank you so much, that's terrific.' He reached into his back pocket for his wallet, extracted several notes and held them out.

She noticed the glint of gold again. He was wearing a signet ring, engraved with a crest and worn on his little finger.

'You will charge extra for all the trouble you've gone to, won't you?' he said.

'Not when it's Christmas.' She sent him a quick smile as she handed him his change.

She expected him to leave then, but he continued to stand there, looking at the bright parcels on the counter with a long distance look in his eyes, as if he were lost in thought.

'Was there something else?' she asked tentatively. She wouldn't mind at all if he wanted to stay longer. Nothing else like him was likely to happen to her this Christmas.

'If only I could take something more exciting, something Ivy would really love,' he said and he glanced behind him to the slightly dusty row of reading material and reached for a comic book. 'What about this?'

*An Action Man comic?* Jo did her best not to look shocked. 'I don't think Ivy's started school yet,' she suggested gently. 'I'd be surprised if she could read.'

He closed his eyes for a moment. 'It would have been so simple to pick up a toy in Sydney. There isn't time to ring a city toy shop and fly something out, is there?'

'Well…no. I shouldn't think so…' Goodness, if he was prepared to hire an aircraft, this must be important. He *must* be Ivy's father—and he must also be a man who made sure he got what he wanted. No wonder a box of chocolates seemed unsatisfactory, even with the pretty wrapping.

'There are no other shops around here?'

'No toy shops, I'm afraid. Not unless you want to backtrack about two hundred kilometres.'

With an air of resignation he began to gather up his parcels, but he moved without haste.

'You really want to make a big impression on Ivy, don't you?' Jo suggested.

He nodded. 'It's vitally important.'

There was an intensity in his voice and a sadness in his eyes that sent an unexpected tiny pain sweeping through her. How awful for him if he was Ivy's father, but had never met his daughter. And where was Ivy's mother? What tragedy had occurred? Jo's own family were very close and her soft heart ached for him.

'Well…thank you very much for all your help,' he said, turning to go.

Oh, crumbs. She felt rotten about sending him away with such inappropriate presents. 'Look,' she said to his back. 'If this present is really important, I might be able to help you.'

He turned and looked at her, his green eyes intense. Fuzzy heat flashed through her.

'I have a mountain of toys that I've bought for my brothers and sisters,' she said. 'Probably more than I'll need. If—if you'd like to take a look at them, you're welcome. We should be able to find some little toy to add to the chocolates.'

His green eyes studied her and she tried to look calm and unaffected, but then he did the crooked smile thing and her insides went crazy.

'That's incredibly kind of you.'

'I'll just call one of my brothers to come and mind the shop,' she said. 'Wait here.' And, before he could protest, she hurried away through a door at the back of the shop.

It led directly into their house.

Down the central hallway she rushed, heading straight for the backyard where she knew from the boys' shouts that they were playing cricket. And with every hasty step she fought off doubts.

She knew it was impulsive, but somehow this was something she had to do. Poor little Ivy deserved a proper Christmas present. And of course spending more time with Ivy's gorgeous father was simply a chore to be endured...

She managed to convince her brother Bill that he

was needed and then she almost ran back through the house. She was a touch breathless as she re-entered the shop.

The Englishman was still there, looking strangely out of place beside a mountain of dried dog food. He seemed to be making polite conversation with old Hilda Bligh, the town gossip.

'There you are, Jo,' said Hilda. 'I was just telling Mr Strickland that if the shop's empty we usually holler until someone comes.'

Goodness, Hilda already knew the man's name. No doubt the old girl had been treated to one of his dangerously attractive smiles.

'Sorry, Mrs Bligh, you know what Christmas Eve can be like. Here's Bill. He'll look after you.'

Jo glanced towards the Englishman, feeling rather foolish because she was about to invite him into her home and she didn't know the first thing about him. 'Can you come this way?' she asked him.

'It was very nice to meet you, Mr Strickland,' called Hilda Bligh, smiling after him coyly.

Jo led the man through the doorway and into the shabby central passage that ran the full length of their house.

'So you're Mr Strickland?' she said once they were clear of the shop.

'Yes, my name's Hugh—Hugh Strickland. And I believe you're Jo.'

Jo nodded.

'Short for Josephine?'

'Joanna.' She held out her hand. 'Joanna Berry.' Somehow it seemed important to shake hands—to make this exchange businesslike. But it wasn't exactly businesslike to have her hand clasped warmly by Hugh Strickland.

'I take it Hilda Bligh filled you in?' she asked.

'Indeed and with astonishing attention to detail.'

She groaned. 'I hate to think what she's told you.'

Hugh smiled. 'I don't think she told me what you scored on your spelling test in the second grade, but I believe I know just about everything else.'

'I'm sorry. Outback towns are so—'

'Exposing?'

Jo nodded her head and sighed. This really was the weirdest situation.

'Yes, well…' She took a deep breath. 'We'd better take a look at these toys. I'm afraid I'm going to have to take you into my bedroom.'

'Really?'

He didn't look shocked—he was too smooth for that—but Jo knew he was surprised. She made a joke of it. 'Of course I don't usually invite strange men into my room within minutes of meeting them.'

Amusement sparkled in his eyes. 'Mrs Bligh didn't mention it.'

Thank heavens he had a sense of humour.

'I've hidden the presents in there, you see, and I can't bring them out or one of the children might find them.' She turned and led him down the passage.

But, despite her matter-of-fact air, she was suddenly nervous. It didn't seem possible that she was actually doing this. She, ordinary, average Jo Berry, was taking a man who was a mixture of every gorgeous British actor she'd ever swooned over into her dreadful bedroom.

It was more than dreadful. She'd taken all her favourite bits and pieces to decorate her flat in Brisbane, so her room was as bare and as ugly as a prison cell.

It held nothing more than a simple iron bed with a worn and faded cover, bare timber floorboards, a scratched, unvarnished nightstand and an ancient wardrobe, once polished silky oak, but painted creamy-orange by her father during one of Mum's decorating drives. The old Holland blind that covered her window was faded with age and had a watermark stain where rain had got in during a storm several summers ago.

'Perhaps this isn't a good idea,' Hugh said. 'I can't take gifts from your family.'

'But isn't it vitally important to have a present for little Ivy?'

'Well…'

Without further hesitation, Jo dragged her suitcase out from under the bed. 'Luckily I haven't wrapped these yet,' she said, looking up at him over her shoulder.

And he was smiling again—that dangerous smile—with his eyes fixed directly on the expanding gap between her T-shirt and her jeans.

Heaving the suitcase on to her bed, she began hauling gifts out to pile on her bedspread.

What she was looking for were the stocking fillers she'd bought to help her mother out—small fluffy toys, plastic spiders, dress-up jewellery, fishing lures, puzzles...

But she more or less had to get everything out because these things were mixed in with the main presents—the action figures and video games for Bill and Eric; the books and CDs for the older boys; the 'magic' magnetic drawing board and hair accessories for Grace and the baby doll for Tilly.

She glanced up at Hugh and felt a pang of dismay when she saw the look in his eyes as he stared at the doll.

As baby dolls went, it was perfect. She'd been thrilled when she'd found it. It came in a little cane carry basket with a pink quilted lining and there was also a feeding bottle and a change of clothes.

'You have quite a treasure trove here,' he said.

'I need to negotiate a bank loan every year just to cope with Christmas,' she joked.

'Six brothers and sisters...'

'Mrs Bligh told you that too?'

He nodded and smiled, then looked back at the bed. 'I'd pay you anything for that doll.'

Jo thought of Ivy. She was such a sweet little thing and for a fleeting moment she almost weakened. But then she came to her senses. 'Sorry. Not possible. That's earmarked for Tilly.' She reached for a fluffy lavender-hued unicorn. 'What about this? Unicorns are all the rage with the pre-school set.'

One dark eyebrow lifted. 'I would never have guessed. I'm completely out of my depth when it comes to little girls.'

'Or there's this—' She reached for some multi-coloured plastic bangles, but stopped when she heard the sound of giggling on the other side of the door. Her stomach plunged.

Tiptoeing to the door, she listened. Yes, there was another burst of giggles.

Carefully, she opened the door a crack and found Tilly and Eric crouching there, their eyes dancing with merriment. 'Get lost, you two.'

'Bill says you've got a man in there,' said Tilly.

'That's none of your business. Now run away.'

Eric bumped against the door as if he wanted to push it open, but Jo blocked it with her hip.

'Is he your boyfriend?' asked Tilly.

'No, of course not. Now scram, both of you!'

Face aflame, Jo slipped back through the narrow opening, slammed the door shut and locked it again. Embarrassed, she rolled her eyes to the ceiling, hardly daring to look at Hugh, but when she did she saw that he was standing in the middle of the room with his hands thrust in his trouser pockets, wearing an expression that was a complicated mixture of amusement and impatience.

'I do appreciate your efforts.' He gallantly remained silent about the antics of her siblings. 'But I think I'd better be off.'

'Yes,' she said. 'Will you take the unicorn?'

'Are you sure you can spare it?'

'Absolutely. Right now, I'd be happy if you took all the presents. I might yet disown my entire family.'

He flashed her a smile. 'Just the unicorn would be terrific, thank you.'

Jo thrust the fluffy toy into a non-see-through pink plastic bag and handed it to him. 'Done.'

As she hastily transferred everything back into the suitcase and dropped the lid, Hugh reached for his wallet again.

'No.' She shook her head. 'No money. It's for Ivy.' Quickly she opened the door.

'I must say I'm terribly grateful to you,' Hugh said. 'I would have hated to turn up at Agate Downs on Christmas Eve without the right gift.'

His smile and his confession, delivered in his beautifully modulated, polite English voice, had the strangest effect on Jo. She had to fight off a weird impulse to bar the door so he couldn't leave.

'Well,' she said, pushing such silliness out of her head and turning briskly businesslike again. 'I mustn't keep you any longer, Mr Strickland. I'm sure you need to be on your way and I'd better relieve Bill in the shop.'

He hurried off then. After delivering one last quick but sincere thank you he made a hasty farewell, heading out the front door in record time.

Leaping into his vehicle, he pulled out from the kerb at the same reckless speed with which he'd arrived.

And Jo was left feeling strangely deflated.

Her thoughts returned to where she'd been before he'd arrived. Remembering her friends at the office Christmas party in the city, all having a ball.

While Hugh Strickland, possibly the dishiest man in the world and as close to Prince Charming as Jo was ever likely to meet, was riding off in his glittering coach—well, OK, his four-wheel drive. Roaring down a bush track.

Never to be seen again.

## CHAPTER TWO

BINDI CREEK had its last-minute pre-Christmas rush shortly after Hugh left. It seemed to Jo that almost every household in the township, as well as some from outlying properties, suddenly remembered that the shop would be closed for the next two days and that they needed items vital for Christmas.

No doubt it was paranoia, but Jo couldn't help wondering if some of them had come to the shop just to spy on her. At least two of the local women hinted—with very unsubtle nudges and winks—that they'd heard from Hilda Bligh about Jo's *special* visitor. One of them actually said that she'd heard the Martens were expecting a visit from Ivy's father.

Jo pretended she had no idea what they were talking about.

Apart from these awkward moments, she was happy to be kept busy. The work kept her mind from straying Hugh-wards.

Brad and Nick, two of her brothers who worked further out west on cattle properties, arrived home around eight. They came into the shop and greeted her with hugs and back slaps and they hung about for ten minutes or so, catching up on her news. Then they went back into the house for the warmed left-over dinner Mum had saved for them.

Jo ate a scratch meal at the counter and she was tired when it was time to close up the shop. She went to lock the front door and looked out into the street and took a few deep breaths. It was a hot, still summer's night and the air felt dry and dusty, but despite this she caught a hint of frangipani and night-scented jasmine drifting from nearby gardens.

Overhead, the Christmas Eve sky was cloudless and clear and splashed with an extravaganza of silver-bright stars. Grace and Tilly would be watching that sky from their bedroom window, hoping for a glimpse of Santa Claus and his reindeer. And Mum would be warning Eric and Bill not to spoil their little sisters' fantasies.

What would little Ivy be doing out at Agate Downs? Had she received her present? Had she liked the lavender unicorn? For a moment Jo let her mind play with the mystery of Hugh Strickland and this child. She could picture him very clearly as he climbed out of his vehicle with the toy unicorn clutched in one hand. Goodness, she should have put it in something more attractive than a plastic bag.

Thinking about him and his mysterious errand caused an unwelcome pang around her heart. She shivered and rubbed her arms to chase away goose-bumps. What was the point of thinking over and over about Hugh? Perhaps she was getting man-crazy. It was six months since she'd broken up with Damien.

She locked the doors, pulled down the blinds, locked the till and turned out the lights in the shop. It was time to slip into her bedroom to wrap her presents. Once the children were safely asleep, she would have fun setting the brightly wrapped gifts under the Christmas tree in the lounge room.

The Berrys enjoyed a no-frills Christmas Eve. She'd have a cup of tea with Mum and they'd both put their feet up. The older boys would sit out on the back veranda with Dad, yarning about cattle and drinking their first icy-cold Christmas beer, while she and Mum talked over their final plans for the festive meals tomorrow.

She hadn't quite completed the gift-wrapping saga when there was a knock on her bedroom door. 'Who is it?' she called softly, not wanting to wake her sisters in the next room.

'It's Mum.'

'Just a minute.' Jo had been wrapping her mother's presents—French perfume and a CD compilation of her mum's favourite music from the sixties and seventies—so she slipped these quickly under her pillow. 'I'm almost finished.'

When she opened the door her mother looked strangely excited. 'You have a visitor.'

'Really? Who is it?'

'An Englishman. He says his name's Hugh Strickland.'

An arrow-swift jolt shot through Jo. 'Are you sure?'

'Of course I'm sure.' Margie Berry's brow wrinkled into a worried frown. 'Who is he, love? He seems very nice and polite, but do you want me to send him away?'

'Oh, no,' Jo answered quickly. 'He's just a customer. He—he was in the shop this afternoon.'

'Yes, he told me that. He said you were very helpful.' Margie looked expectant, but Jo was reluctant to go into details.

Her mind raced. Why was Hugh here? He was supposed to be at Agate Downs. 'W-where is he?'

'I found him on the back veranda, talking to Dad and the boys, but it's you he wants. He asked for you ever so politely, so I told him to wait in the kitchen.'

'The kitchen?' Her bedroom had been bad enough and Jo winced when she tried to picture Hugh Strickland in their big old out-of-date kitchen, cluttered this evening with the aftermath of Mum's Christmas baking. Somehow the image wouldn't gel.

Jo was gripping the door handle so hard her hand ached as she let it go. This didn't make sense. 'Did you ask him why he wants to see me?'

Margie gave an irritated toss of her head. 'No, I didn't.'

Jo wished she had a chance to check her appearance in the mirror, but her mother was waiting with her hands on her hips and a knowing glint in her eyes. Besides, what was the point of titivating? Hugh Strickland had already seen her today and she would look much the same as she had earlier. Her smooth brown hair was cut into a jaw-length bob that never seemed to get very untidy and she wasn't wearing make-up, and there wasn't much she could do to improve her plain white T-shirt and blue jeans.

Just the same, she felt nervous as she set off down the passage for the kitchen, as if she were going to an audition for a part in a play but had no idea what role she was trying for.

Hugh was standing near the scrubbed pine table in the middle of the room and the moment she saw him she went all weak-kneed and breathless.

And that was *before* he smiled.

Oh, heavens, he *was* good-looking. She'd been beginning to wonder if perhaps her imagination had exaggerated how gorgeous he was.

No way. His dark hair was still spiky, but that was part of his appeal, as was the five o'clock shadow that darkened his strong jaw line. And beyond that there was a subtle air of superiority about him—a matter of breeding perhaps, something unmistakable like the born-to-win lines of a well-bred stallion.

But behind his charming smile she could sense banked-up emotion carefully held in check. What was it? Anger? Impatience? Dismay?

She wondered if she should ask him to sit down, but his tension suggested he'd rather stand. Why had he returned so soon?

He answered that question immediately when he held out the pink plastic bag she'd given him. 'I came to return this.'

Frowning, Jo accepted it. She could feel the shape of the fluffy unicorn still inside. Her mind raced, trying to work out what this could mean. 'Couldn't you find your way to Agate Downs?'

'I found the place,' he said. 'Your directions were spot on.'

'So what happened? Weren't the Martens home?'

'I turned back without seeing them.' A muscle worked in his jaw and he dropped his gaze. His face seemed to stiffen. 'I had second thoughts. It's the wrong time.'

'Oh.' What else could she say? This was none of her business. 'That's a—a pity.' A few hours ago it had been vitally important that Hugh made a good impression on the child. And it had seemed important that it happened *today*. Jo pressed her lips together, fighting the impulse to interrogate him.

He looked up briefly and she caught a stronger flash of emotion in his intense gaze before he looked away again. Was it anger? 'I didn't want to spoil Ivy's Christmas. I—I mean—her guardians knew that I was on my way, but I realised it would be intrusive.'

She wondered how Hugh Strickland would react if he knew that the locals were gossiping about him.

His eyes sought hers again. 'I suddenly thought how it would be for Ivy to have a strange man turning up on her doorstep on Christmas Eve, claiming—' He broke off in mid-sentence.

*Claiming…what?* Jo's tense hands tightened around the package and the unicorn let out a sharp squeak. She was so uptight that she jumped.

'So what will you do now?' she asked.

'I've found a room at the pub.'

'Oh…good.'

'I'll stay there till Christmas is over and I'll go back to the Martens' place on Boxing Day.'

Jo thrust the unicorn back into his hands. 'If you're still hoping to see Ivy, you must keep this. You'll need it.'

Their hands were touching now, and as they both held the package she was exquisitely aware of Hugh's strong, warm fingers covering hers.

'No,' he said. 'I came here tonight because I wanted to give this back to you in time for your family's Christmas. There won't be the same pressing urgency for a gift for Ivy once Christmas is over. And this was really meant for one of your sisters.'

He was looking directly into her eyes and making her heart pound.

Their gazes remained linked for longer than was necessary, and Jo knew she would always remember the shimmering intimacy of his green eyes as he looked at her then and the heated touch of his hands on hers.

It was almost depressing to realise that memories of this handsome stranger were going to haunt her nights and linger in her daydreams…for ages into the future…

'Please keep the unicorn.' She felt so breathless her voice was hardly more than a whisper. 'Believe me, little girls always like presents.'

He sent her a quick smile. 'If you insist. I'll trust your deep understanding of what little girls like. The only one I know well is my goddaughter, but she's only six months old, so our communication has been somewhat limited.'

'Believe me, where presents are concerned, little girls are no different from big girls; they never get tired of receiving gifts.'

His eyes flashed confident amusement.

'But I'm sure you already know that.'

'Indeed.'

But then he seemed to remember something else and almost immediately his smile faded.

And the spell that had kept their hands linked was broken. Jo stepped back, leaving him with the unicorn, and Hugh looked away.

She drew a quick nervous breath. *Calm down, Jo. Stay cool. You're getting overheated about nothing. Nothing. He hasn't come back to see you and he'll be leaving again any moment now.*

'There's another thing I wanted to ask you, Jo,' he said softly.

Her head jerked up.

'I wonder if I can possibly impose on you one more time?'

Caught by surprise, she found herself blustering. 'How? W-what would you like me to do?'

'I want you to come with me when I go back to Agate Downs.'

*Crumbs.* 'Why me? I don't understand.'

'You already know Ivy—and you have so many brothers and sisters. I have no experience with young children. I can't even remember what it's like to be five.'

She tried to speak as casually as he had. 'So you think I can help you somehow?'

A muscle in his throat worked. 'Yes—if you could spare the time. I get the impression you've hit it off with Ivy already.'

'I'm afraid I'm not an expert at managing small children,' she warned him. 'You've seen how naughty Tilly can be.'

'But you're used to them. You're relaxed around them.'

'Well…' Jo's immediate impulse was to help him, but a nagging inner warning was hard to ignore. 'It might be helpful if I understood a little more about this situation,' she said carefully.

He nodded and then he looked directly into her eyes again. 'The situation's quite straightforward really. Ivy's my daughter.'

Right. Jo tried to swallow. So now she knew for sure. Did this mean Hugh was married? She glanced at his hands. The only ring he wore was the signet ring on the little finger of his left hand.

Sensing the direction of her gaze, he smiled wryly, lifted his hand and waggled his bare fourth finger. 'No, I'm not married. I only dated my daughter's mother for a while. And...her mother is dead.'

'Oh, how sad.' This changed everything. All at once Jo was adrift on a sea of sympathy. She said quickly, 'Why don't we sit down for a bit?'

He pulled out a wooden chair on the other side of the kitchen table. 'If I'm asking you to help with Ivy I should be perfectly honest with you,' he said. 'I only learned of her existence a short time ago.'

Jo watched the barely perceptible squaring of his shoulders and she sensed that he was working very hard to keep his emotions under control. 'That must have been a terrible shock.' Her kind-hearted urges were going into overdrive now. 'How come you only learned about Ivy recently?'

Hugh stiffened and she guessed she was delving deeper than he wanted to go. But he met her gaze. 'Her mother wrote a letter but it never reached me and she died shortly after Ivy's birth.'

Jo thought of the dear little bright-eyed Ivy who'd danced about their shop like a winsome fairy while her guardian had selected groceries. How sad that her mother never knew her.

How sad that Hugh still hadn't met her. Jo blinked away the threat of tears.

'It gets worse.' Hugh spoke very quietly. 'Apparently Linley suffered from severe postnatal depression and—and she committed suicide.'

'No!' A horrified exclamation burst from Jo. 'I'm so sorry,' she added quickly. Then she asked gently, 'And you never knew?'

'I thought she had died in a car accident,' he said. 'There was never any mention of a baby.'

Jo wondered if he was being so forthright to draw her into the task of helping him. Well, it was working. It would be hard to turn him down now, especially when his eyes held hers with such compelling intensity.

'Ivy's grandmother died recently and she left instructions in her will, demanding that I claim my daughter,' he said. 'Of course I wanted to do the right thing by the child, so I came dashing over here. But I've realised now that my timing is off. On Christmas Eve children are expecting Santa Claus, not strange men claiming to be their father.'

'Ivy might like you better than Santa Claus,' Jo suggested gently.

He sent her a sharp, searching look. 'So you think I've done the wrong thing?'

Jo gulped. This gorgeous, confident man was acting as if he really needed her advice. She sent him an encouraging grin. 'No, I'm sure you've made the right decision. I always believe it's best to follow your instincts.'

'So will you come with me when I collect Ivy?'

Her instincts screamed yes and Jo didn't hesitate to take her own advice.

'Of course I will. I've got a real soft spot for Ivy and, as you said, with six younger brothers and sisters I've got to be something of an expert with kids.'

'Absolutely.' Hugh glanced at the clock on the wall near the stove and jumped to his feet. 'It's getting late and I've taken up far too much of your time.'

Jo wondered if she should warn him about Ivy's scars, but perhaps that would only make him more anxious about meeting her. Or maybe he already knew. It might be best not to make a big deal about them.

Standing, she shoved her hands into the back pockets of her jeans and shrugged in an effort to look unconcerned. 'So we have a date for Boxing Day?'

He nodded stiffly. 'Thanks. I'd really appreciate your help.'

Then he turned and walked to the kitchen door. Jo followed.

'I hope you'll be comfortable at the pub,' she said as they stepped into the hallway. 'It's not very flash.'

'It looks perfectly adequate.'

'A bit lonely for Christmas.'

'I'll be fine.' Suddenly he looked very English, sort of stiff upper lipped and uncomfortable, as if he couldn't stand sentimental females who made fusses about Christmas.

Her mother appeared in the hall. 'Did I hear you say you're staying at the pub, Mr Strickland?'

Jo wanted to cringe at her mother's intrusion, but Hugh didn't seem to mind.

'Yes. It's basic but quite adequate.'

'You're not having Christmas dinner there, are you?'

'They've booked me in. Why? Is there a problem?'

'Oh, not the pub for Christmas.' Margie sounded shocked and she thumped her hands on her hips in a gesture of indignation. 'We can't let you do that.'

'I'm sure the food will be fine.' Hugh was beginning to sound defensive now. 'I'm told they do a fine roast turkey.'

'But you'll be all on your own. At Christmas.'

Jo could tell where this was heading, but it would look a bit weird if she suddenly leapt to Hugh's rescue by insisting that he would be fine at the pub.

'And you're so far from home,' her mother said. 'No, Mr Strickland, I won't hear of it. You must join us tomorrow. I know we're not flash, but at least there's a crowd of us. You won't feel lonely here and we're going to have plenty of food. I hate to think of anyone being alone at Christmas.'

Hugh's expression was circumspect—a polite mask—and Jo waited for him to excuse himself with his characteristic, well-mannered graciousness.

But to her amazement, he said, 'That's very kind of you, Mrs Berry. Thank you, I'd love to come.'

*     *     *

Hugh arrived punctually at noon the next day, bearing two beautifully chilled bottles of champagne.

Jo's dad, who drank beer, eyed them dubiously, but her mum was effusive.

'Nothing like a glass of bubbles to make the day special,' she said, beaming at him. 'But don't let me have any till I've got all the food on the table or I'll forget to serve something. Nick,' she called to her eldest son, 'can you find a bucket and fill it with ice? We don't want to let these bottles warm up and there's not a speck of room in the fridge.'

Jo had given herself several stern lectures while getting ready that morning. She'd chosen a cool summery dress of fine white cotton edged with dainty lace, and she'd applied her make-up with excruciating care. But, in spite of her efforts to look her best, she was determined to stay calm and unaffected by Hugh's visit.

She was so busy helping her mother to get all the food out of the kitchen and on to the table that she had to leave Hugh to the tender mercies of her father and brothers, but she heard snatches of their conversation as she went back and forth.

'Hugh Strickland,' said her dad. 'Your name rings a bell. Should I have heard of you?'

'I shouldn't think so.'

'What line of work are you in?'

'I'm in business—er—transport.'

'In the UK?'

'That's right.'

Her dad mumbled knowingly. 'I almost got a job in transport once—driving buses—but I wasn't fit for it. My chest was crushed, you see. Mining accident. Lungs punctured, so they pensioned me off.'

Hugh made sympathetic noises.

Jo chewed her lip and wondered if she should try to butt in and change the conversation. Her dad tended to carry on a bit.

But if Hugh was bored, he showed no sign. He was fitting in like a local. Clutching his beer in its inelegant Styrofoam cooler, he relaxed in a squatter's chair and looked surprisingly comfortable.

The family always gathered for Christmas lunch on a screened-in veranda shaded by an ancient mango tree. This was the cool side of the house, but Jo wondered if an Englishman would realise that. It was still very hot, even in the shade.

'Now, Hugh,' said Mum after everyone had found a place to sit and the family had been through the ritual of pulling crackers and donning unbecoming paper hats. 'You'll see we don't have a hot dinner.'

'That's perfectly understandable.' Hugh smiled bravely from beneath a pink and purple crêpe paper crown, which should have made him look foolish but somehow managed to look perfectly fine.

Her mum waved a full glass of champagne towards the table. 'There's four different kinds of salad and there's sliced leg ham, cold roast pork and our pièce de résistance is the platter of prawns and bugs.'

'Bugs?' Hugh looked a tad worried.

'Moreton Bay bugs,' Jo hastened to explain, pointing to the platter in the table's centre. 'They're a type of crayfish. If you like seafood, you'll love these.'

Hugh did like them. Very much. In fact he loved everything on the table and ate as much seafood and salad as her brothers, which was saying something. And then he found room to sample the mince pies.

And, not surprisingly, he was an expert dinner party guest, an interesting conversationalist, who also encouraged Nick and Brad to regale them all with hilarious accounts of the antics of the ringers on the cattle stations where they worked. And he enjoyed listening while the younger children chimed in with their stories too.

Knowing how tense Hugh had been yesterday, Jo was surprised by how relaxed he seemed now. No doubt he was charming her family to ensure her commitment to helping him.

She decided to relax. She'd been working hard all year in the city and had put in long hours in the shop during the past week and now she decided to let go a little and to enjoy the fine icy champagne. How in heaven's name had Hugh unearthed such lovely French champagne in the Bindi Creek pub?

Everyone raved about Jo's Christmas pudding of brandy-flavoured ice cream filled with dried fruit, nuts and cherries and afterwards her mum announced that she was going to have a little lie down. And everyone agreed that was exactly what she deserved.

'Jo, you take Hugh out on to the back veranda for

coffee,' she suggested, 'while this mob gets cracking in the kitchen.'

With coffee cups in hand, Jo and Hugh retired to the veranda. They leant against the railing, looking out over the tops of straggly plumbago bushes to the sunburnt back paddock and it was good to stand and stretch for a while; Jo felt she had eaten and drunk too much.

The air was warm and slightly sticky and it hung about them like a silent and invisible veil. Jo would have liked to run down to the creek, to shed her clothes and take a dip in the cool green water. She'd done it often before, in private, but she found herself wondering what it would be like to skinny-dip with Hugh. The very thought sent her heartbeats haywire.

They didn't speak at first and she felt a bit self-conscious to be alone with him again after sharing him with her noisy family. The slanting rays of the afternoon sun lit up the dark hair above his right ear, lending it a gilded sheen and highlighting his cheekbone and one side of his rather aristocratic nose.

Eventually he said, 'Your family are fascinating, aren't they?'

'Do you really think so? It must be rather overpowering to meet them all in one fell swoop.'

He smiled as he shook his head. 'I think you're very lucky to have grown up with such a happy brood. They're so relaxed.'

She shrugged. 'They have their moments. Christmas is always fun.'

'I'm impressed that they'll take in a stranger, knowing next to nothing about him.'

Too true, she thought. Hugh had shared rather personal details about Ivy in his bid to enlist her help, but she knew next to nothing about the rest of his life.

'You don't come from a big family?' she asked.

'Not in terms of brothers and sisters. I'm an only child. I guess that's why I'm always fascinated by big families.'

'Sometimes I envy only children. It would be nice, now and then, to have that kind of privacy. Then again, I spend most of my time these days working in the city.'

His right eyebrow lifted, forming a question mark, but, unlike her, he didn't give voice to his curiosity, so there was an awkward moment where they were both aware that the rhythm of their conversation had tripped.

Hugh stood staring into the distance.

'Are you thinking about Ivy?' Jo asked.

At first he seemed a little startled by her question, but then he smiled. 'How did you guess?'

'Feminine intuition.' She drained her coffee cup. 'Seriously, it must have come as a shock to have a five-year-old dropped into your life.'

'It was a shock all right.' Taking a final sip of coffee, he set his empty cup and saucer on a nearby table and, with his usual gentlemanly manners, he took Jo's cup and set it there too.

'I feel so unprepared for meeting Ivy,' he said. 'I don't like being unprepared. How the hell does a bachelor suddenly come to terms with caring for a child?'

'He hires a nanny?'

'Well, yes,' he admitted with a wry grimace. 'A nanny will be essential. But I'll still have to do the whole fatherhood thing.'

'At least Ivy's not a baby. She can talk to you and express her needs. I'm sure you'll become great mates with her.'

'Mates?' He couldn't have looked more stunned if she'd suggested that Ivy would take over as CEO of his business.

'Good friends,' she amended.

'With a five-year-old little girl?'

Jo thought of the warm lifelong friendship she'd shared with her mum. 'Why not?'

Hugh shook his head. 'A boy might have been easier. At least I have inside knowledge of how little boys tick.'

'Don't be sexist. There are lots of little girls who like the same things as boys. Grace and Tilly love to play cricket and go fishing. So do I, for that matter.'

'Do you?' He regarded her with a look that was both amused and delighted, but then he frowned and with his elbows resting on the veranda railing he stared down into the plumbago bush. 'But what if Ivy turns on a horrendous scene? It would be horrible if she cried all the way home on the flight back to London.'

'Goodness,' cried Jo. 'You're a walking advertisement for the power of positive thinking, aren't you?'

For a moment he looked put out, and then he smiled. 'You're right. I'm normally on top of things, so I guess I should be able to handle this.' He sent Jo an extra devilish smile. 'With a little expert help.'

*Gulp.* 'Just remember Ivy is your flesh and blood,' she said. 'She's probably a chip off the old block.'

'Which would mean she's charming and well-mannered, even-tempered, good-looking and highly intelligent.'

'You missed conceited.'

Hugh chuckled softly and then he glanced up and seemed suddenly fascinated by something above her head. 'Is that mistletoe hanging above you?'

Jo tipped her head back. Sure enough there was a bunch of greenery dangling from a hook in the veranda roof. 'I can probably blame one of my brothers for that.' She rolled her eyes, trying to make light of it, but as she looked at Hugh again his smile lingered and something about it sent shivers skittering through her.

How silly. This reserved Englishman had no intention of kissing her. And, even if he did, why should she get all shivery at the thought of a quick Christmas peck?

But her jumping insides paid absolutely no attention to such common sense.

Hugh gave an easy shrug of his shoulders and his eyes held hers as he murmured ever so softly in his super-sexy English voice, 'Tradition is terribly important, Jo. And you're under the mistletoe and it *is* Christmas.'

Her stomach began a drum roll.

# CHAPTER THREE

SOMETHING deep and dark in Hugh's gaze made Jo's pulses leap to frantic life.

*Oh, for heaven's sake, calm down, girl.*

Why was she getting so worked up about a friendly Christmas kiss?

*Because Hugh is gorgeous!*

She took a step closer to him and Hugh's hand cupped her elbow as if to support her. She hoped he didn't notice that she was trembling.

And then, without warning, he dipped his head. 'Happy Christmas, Jo.'

She pursed her lips for a quick peck and let her body tilt forward. But the anticipated peck didn't take place.

Instead Hugh's lips settled warmly on hers and suddenly he was kissing her. Properly. Or she was kissing him? It no longer mattered. All that mattered was that it was a full-on kiss.

She could blame the champagne. Or the heat. No, she would blame Hugh, because he was far too gorgeous and far too expert at kissing. There had to be some logical reason to explain how a simple mistletoe kiss became so thorough and lasted for such a long and lovely time.

Yes, she would blame Hugh because at some point his hands slipped around her waist, and then it was incredibly easy and seemed perfectly OK to nestle in against him. His arms bound her close against his strong, intensely masculine body and his mouth, tasting faintly of coffee, delved hers expertly and with daring intimacy.

Without warning, a flood of unexpected yearning washed over her. Her insides went into meltdown. Soft, hungry little sounds rumbled low in her throat as she pushed closer into Hugh.

Oh, man. Never had she experienced a kiss that was so instantly shattering.

The sound of footsteps brought her plummeting back to earth. With a little whimper of disappointment, she broke away.

Hugh let her go and he stood very still with his shoulders squared and his hands by his sides, watching her intently and not quite smiling. Only his accelerated breathing betrayed that he'd been as aroused by the kiss as she had.

Taking a deep breath, Jo shot a scowl back over her shoulder to see who'd interrupted them.

It was Bill and Eric and their mouths were hanging wide open.

'What's eating you two?' she demanded angrily. 'Haven't you ever seen someone get kissed under the mistletoe before?'

Eric's face was sheepish. 'Not like that.'

'Get lost,' she said, feeling flustered. 'Finish those dishes.'

They vanished. Which left her with Hugh, who'd gone quiet again. In fact he was looking so uncomfortable that she wondered suddenly if he regretted the kiss. Damn him. He'd probably only kissed her to get closer to her—to ensure that she would accompany him to Agate Downs.

But he'd been so passionate, so *involved*.

Good grief. She was trying to read too much into the kiss. Hugh had simply reacted to the Christmas tradition. And she'd been carried away. Look how calm he was now.

Nevertheless, their easy conversation was over. They carried their coffee cups back to the kitchen and soon afterwards Hugh said polite farewells and set off for the pub. He left without any special word for Jo.

She was left to be plagued by annoying doubts. And no matter how many times she told herself to be sensible, confusion about the passion in Hugh's kiss kept her churning for the rest of Christmas Day.

Hugh was nervous.

He hated feeling nervous. It was so alien to his nature. Normally he was always in control, but in all his adult life he couldn't remember feeling so helpless.

As he drove with Jo to Agate Downs, he had to keep taking deep, slow breaths to remain calm. Even so, emotion clogged his throat and he kept swallowing to be rid of it.

Jo seemed subdued too, and he wondered if she was remembering the kiss they'd shared yesterday. The chemistry of it had been rather sobering. It had caught him completely by surprise. He'd anticipated a harmless exchange beneath the mistletoe and had found himself launching a fully-fledged seduction.

He might have taken things beyond the point of sanity if her brothers hadn't arrived on the scene.

The rough outback track reached a rusty old iron gate where Hugh had turned back two days ago. Jo pushed open the passenger door. 'I'll get the gate.'

About ten minutes later, after they'd traversed a long paddock dotted with rather scrawny-looking cattle, the homestead emerged through the trees.

Jo frowned. 'I haven't been out here for years. This place is looking very run-down, isn't it?'

Hugh nodded. He tried to picture his daughter living here. The yard around the homestead was weedy and parched, with no sign of a garden, and as far as he could see there weren't any playthings to amuse a child—no tricycle and no swing hanging from the old jacaranda tree.

He felt a rush of adrenalin as he parked the car. Within a matter of minutes he would see Ivy, the unknown daughter he was to take home with him, the child he must adjust his whole life to accommodate.

He no longer doubted that he wanted her. Since

he'd learned of her existence he'd developed an astonishing deep-seated longing to see her and at some unfathomable soul-level he knew he already loved her.

But who was she? And how would she react to him?

Jo touched him on the shoulder and, when he turned, she handed him the unicorn, wrapped now in brightly coloured Christmas paper and topped by a crimson bow sprinkled with silver glitter.

'Don't worry about this, Hugh,' she said. 'Just be yourself. Believe me, Ivy is a very lucky little girl to have a father like you. She'll love you.'

A grim smile was the best he could offer.

At the front door they were greeted by a dark scowl beneath thick bushy eyebrows. Noel Marten stared glumly at Hugh. 'You must be Strickland.'

'Yes.' Hugh extended his hand. 'How do you do?'

'Hmm,' was all Noel Marten said and his hand-shake was noticeably reluctant.

'I telephoned to say I'd be here on Boxing Day,' Hugh added.

'Who is it?' called a voice from deep inside the house.

Noel called over his shoulder. 'It's him— Strickland.'

'Oh.' Ellen Marten came hurrying down the central passage, wiping her damp hands on an apron.

Behind her, at the far end of the passage, a small,

impish figure peered around a doorway. Hugh's throat constricted. There she was. Ivy. His little girl.

Jo reached for his hand and gave it an encouraging squeeze.

'Do come in, sir,' said Ellen Marten, but then she glanced at Jo and looked a little confused.

Jo beamed at her. 'Hi, Ellen. I don't suppose you were expecting me. Hugh's been telling me how excited he is about meeting his daughter at last.' She offered both the Martens her warmest smile.

'I invited Jo because she knows Ivy and she's had much more experience than I have with children,' Hugh explained rather stiffly.

'Right,' said Ellen, nodding slowly.

The far end of the hallway was quite shadowy, but when Hugh glanced that way again he saw the silhouette of a little girl jigging with excitement. His heart began to pound. The child's mother had been beautiful with a slim, pale fragility, luminous brown eyes and a halo of soft, golden hair.

Whose looks had Ivy inherited?

Ellen followed his glance back down the hallway. 'The little monkey; I told her to wait in the kitchen.'

'I don't want to wait,' shouted a very bossy little voice.

Ellen sighed. 'I'm afraid she's quite a little miss. There are times when I don't know what to do with her.'

'That's because you won't listen to me,' growled Noel. 'I know exactly what she needs.'

By now the little girl had sidled along the wall until she was halfway down the passage. She was wearing a pink gingham sundress and no shoes. A handful of pebbles lodged in Hugh's throat. He could see that her hair was a mop of curls as dark as his and she had a pale heart-shaped face with big, expressive eyes—green eyes that were dancing with mischief.

Her nose, mouth and chin were exceptionally dainty and feminine. Strong dark eyebrows and lashes gave her character, as did the intelligence shining in her eyes. He felt an astonishing surge of pride. She was his daughter. She was wonderful.

Ellen called to her, 'Come on then, Ivy. Come and meet your visitor.'

*Your father,* Hugh wanted to add, but he held his tongue. He stood very still, feeling terrified and trying very hard to smile, but not quite managing.

As if sensing his tension, the little girl came to a standstill. She pressed herself against the wall with her hands behind her back and she let her head droop to one side, suddenly shy.

'Come on now, Ivy,' Ellen Marten said sharply. 'Don't keep the man waiting.'

'No.' Ivy pouted. 'Won't come.'

Hugh's stomach sank. Ivy didn't want to meet him and he had no idea how to entice her. No doubt his friends in London would be amused by the fact that he, who could charm twenty-five-year-old females with effortless ease, had no idea how to win the heart of this five-year-old.

Ellen rolled her eyes and sighed again. Noel brandished a fist in the air and Hugh cast a desperate glance in Jo's direction.

And Jo, bless her, was the only person in the room who seemed quite free from anxiety. She flashed a cheery grin across the room to the child. 'Hi there, Ivy.'

'Hello,' came the almost sulky reply.

'I've brought you a special visitor.'

Ivy listened carefully, but she didn't budge.

'Don't you want to come and see the lovely Christmas present Hugh has brought for you?'

'What Christmas present?' Ivy inched forward a step.

'This one,' said Hugh nervously as he held out the bright package. Then, copying Jo's example, he squatted beside her.

'What is it?' asked Ivy, coming closer by cautious degrees.

Hugh hesitated and looked again to Jo. He had no idea about the proper protocol for divulging the contents of gifts to children.

But Jo didn't hesitate. 'It's a beautiful unicorn.'

Ivy came still closer. 'What's a unicorn?' she asked.

'It's like a pony,' said Jo. 'A magic pony.'

That did the trick. Ivy closed the gap.

Hugh was transfixed. Here she was—his flesh and

blood daughter, perfect in every way, with his hair colour and his green eyes. And ten neat little pink toes.

'Are you going to open this?' His husky voice betrayed his emotion and he was sure there were tears in his eyes.

Little Ivy stood staring at the package with her hands clasped behind her back. Her eyes shone with curiosity, but she shook her head. 'You open it.'

'OK.' Hugh began to rip at the paper and his daughter leaned close, her face a pretty picture of concentration. And, as the paper fell away, the unicorn was revealed in all its fluffy lilac glory.

Ivy's eyes widened. 'Is it really magic?'

'Ahh…' Hugh had no idea how to answer her.

Jo came to his rescue. 'See this?' she said, patting the pearly horn on the unicorn's head. 'This is what makes it magic.'

One little hand came out and Ivy touched the tip of the horn with a pink forefinger. 'How is it magic?'

'It brought your daddy to you,' said Jo.

If it was possible Ivy's eyes grew rounder and she looked at Hugh. 'You're my daddy, aren't you?'

He was bewitched, his eyes locked with hers. Ivy was a miracle.

Jo dug him in the ribs with her elbow and he remembered his daughter's question.

'Yes,' he said, swallowing hard. 'I'm your daddy.' Then, balancing on his knees, he leaned forward and kissed her very gently on her soft pink cheek.

Beside him Jo made a low snuffling sound that was suspiciously like a sob.

'Give your unicorn a hug,' she suggested in a very choked-up voice.

A dimple bloomed in the little girl's cheek as she smiled with excitement and then her arms came out to embrace the unicorn. And that was when Hugh saw…her left arm.

*Oh, dear God.* The little girl's arm had obviously been very badly burned and it was a mass of terrible scar tissue from her shoulder to her wrist. Some areas were bright pink and shiny and others were a heart-breaking criss-cross of thickened lesions.

A ragged cry burst from him. How in hell's name had this happened? Rioting emotions stormed him. Without a care for the surprised bystanders, he swept Ivy into his arms and hugged her and the unicorn to his chest. Then, cradling her close, he scrambled to his feet.

With his cheek pressed close to Ivy's, he squeezed his eyes tightly closed to stem the threat of tears and he kissed his daughter's cheek and then her hair.

'My little girl,' he whispered.

His heart almost burst when Ivy flung her little arms around his neck.

'My daddy,' she said softly and then she kissed his cheek.

Behind him, Hugh heard Jo's happy sigh of relief.

'I must say I've never seen her take to anyone so quick,' Ellen remarked.

Almost reluctantly, Hugh lowered Ivy back to the floor and then he turned to Jo. 'I need to speak with the Martens,' he said. 'Would you mind entertaining Ivy for a few minutes?'

'Not at all,' she said brightly. 'Come on, Ivy, let's take your unicorn for a flying lesson.'

As they left, Hugh took a deep breath and directed a searching look at the Martens. 'Right,' he said. 'I want straight answers. I want to know exactly what happened to Ivy. I need to know where and why, and I insist on knowing what's being done about it.'

For the first time in days he felt he was back in control.

When it was time to say goodbye to the Martens, Jo felt that they'd been genuinely very fond of the child, despite Noel's gruffness and Ellen's admission that caring for Ivy really was becoming too much for her. And, although they had prepared themselves and Ivy for the parting, they had shed tears at the farewell.

But the bonding between Hugh and his daughter was the real surprise. There was no problem about Ivy leaving. In fact she was excited about going away with her newfound father.

Now, as they bumped down the track back to Bindi Creek, Jo patted the unicorn. 'So, what are you going to call this fellow?' she asked in her brightest manner.

Ivy, who was sitting between Jo and Hugh, frowned and studied the fluffy animal carefully, turning it over and upside down. 'Is my unicorn a boy or a girl?'

Over Ivy's head, Jo and Hugh exchanged amused glances. 'What would you like it to be?'

Ivy giggled and rolled her expressive eyes as she gave this deep consideration. 'I think he's a boy. Like Daddy.'

'So do I,' said Jo. 'And now you can give him a nice boy's name.'

'Hugh?'

'Well…it might be confusing if Daddy and the unicorn both share the same name.'

'What about Howard?' suggested Hugh.

'Howard?' Jo gave a scoffing laugh. 'For a little girl's toy?'

'I like Howard,' insisted Ivy. 'I want to call my unicorn Howard.'

Hugh sent Jo a smug wink. 'You see? I know more about naming toys than you realised.'

'Howard he is then,' Jo replied with a wry smile.

Ivy grinned up at Hugh and her little face was a glowing picture of adoration.

Jo wanted to cry for them. It was just so sweet the way Hugh and Ivy were so delighted with each other.

By the time they reached Bindi Creek's main street Ivy had nodded off with her head resting against Jo's shoulder.

'Would you like to bring her back to my place?' Jo asked. 'It mightn't be very suitable for her at the pub.'

'I've imposed on your family too much.' He glanced at the sleeping Ivy, still clutching Howard. 'But I know what you mean about the pub. I'm sure a child would be much happier at your place.'

'She wouldn't be any trouble. We can put up a little stretcher bed in the girls' room. She'd love it.'

Hugh smiled just a little sadly. 'She might love it too much. I might never be able to drag her away in the morning.'

'Oh, I hadn't thought of that.' Jo thought about it now and was hit by an unexpected deluge of sadness. She'd been trying not to dwell on the fact that Hugh and Ivy would soon disappear from her life. 'I guess you'll want to try to book a flight home,' she said.

'That's already arranged.'

'Really?' He must have organised it during one of the dozen calls he'd made from Agate Downs on his cellphone. 'So when are you going back to England?' She tried to sound casual, as if she didn't actually care, but she wasn't successful.

'Tomorrow.'

'Heavens.' *For crying out loud, Jo, don't sound so disappointed.* 'You were lucky to get a flight so quickly.'

'I know people in the industry.'

'Oh, yes, of course. I forgot you're in the transport business. So do you get mates' rates?'

'A-ah, yes, something like that.'

'Well, don't worry about Ivy,' she said with a brave smile. 'She already adores you and she understands she's going to England with you. She'll be fine.'

Hugh reached his hand past Ivy and gave hers a squeeze. 'Thanks, Jo.'

She tried to smile.


Tilly and Grace had seen Ivy a few times when she'd been in the shop but they'd never spoken, so they were a little overawed when the beautiful little girl arrived with Jo and Hugh. But their surprise didn't stop them from asking awkward questions.

'What happened to your arm?' Tilly asked almost immediately and Jo wanted to gag her.

But Ivy was matter-of-fact. 'It got burned.'

'Does it hurt?'

'Not really. Not any more. It just looks different, that's all.'

'I asked Santa for a unicorn,' Tilly said next. 'But I got a baby doll instead. Do you want to see her?'

After that, the children got on with the fun of dressing up and playing with Howard and the doll and Ivy was in seventh heaven.

In the kitchen, Hugh said to Jo, 'How private are we here? Is this conversation likely to be overheard?'

'Very likely, I'm afraid.' She wondered what he wanted to discuss.

'Do you think you could come up to the pub with me, for a quick drink and a chat?'

She made the mistake of looking into his eyes and she felt a swift ache deep inside, which warned her that she shouldn't go anywhere near the pub—or anywhere else—with him.

For Hugh, taking her to the pub was a purely practical arrangement—probably to discuss something about Ivy. While she—fool that she was—would be madly wishing it could be a date. And that was crazy.

Then again, what good reason could she give for refusing to go?

'I'll ask Mum to keep an eye on Ivy for us,' she said.

They found a table in a corner of the tiny beer garden, tucked between the side of the pub and the butcher's shop, and covered by a green shade cloth that did little to relieve them from the sweltering heat.

'You'll be pleased to get back to England's winter,' Jo said, pressing her cool glass against her face and neck.

Hugh chuckled. 'Give me two days in gloomy London in late December and I'll wish I was back here.'

'So you live in London?'

'Yes. I have a house in Chelsea.'

'Chelsea? That's a very nice area, isn't it?'

'It's quite nice. Very central, handy for everything.'

Jo realised how very little she knew about this man, while he knew so much about her; he'd even been inside her bedroom.

'So,' she said, after she'd taken a deep sip of wine, 'what did you want to talk about?'

'Ivy,' he said simply.

Of course. Jo sent him her warmest smile. 'She's a darling.'

'She is, isn't she?'

'Absolutely. She's bright and spirited, with the potential to be naughty, I'm sure, but she's incredibly sweet and beautiful.'

Hugh smiled and then his face grew sombre. 'I thought my heart was going to break when I saw the scars from her burns.'

Ellen Marten had told Jo about Ivy's burns as the two women had packed the last of Ivy's belongings. At the age of two Ivy had been living at her grandmother's Point Piper mansion in Sydney where Ellen and Noel had been servants, and somehow she'd escaped from her nanny and toddled into the kitchen where she'd pulled a pot of boiling water from the stove.

She'd spent a lot of time in hospital and had had several skin grafts.

Jo reached across the table and laid her hand on his. 'Ivy will be OK, Hugh. She has you now. Don't feel too sorry for her. You're going to be a wonderful father. She's a very lucky little girl.'

'I'll make sure she has the very best medical attention. Luckily, I have an old school friend who's a top burns specialist.'

Hugh looked at her hand covering his and something in his expression made Jo suddenly nervous. She retracted her hand and picked up her wineglass.

Hugh stared hard at the white froth on the top of his beer. 'I want you to come back to London with us,' he said.

Her heart took off like a racing car.

'I know this is short notice and probably very inconvenient, but I would pay you well. The thing is, Ivy's obviously expecting you to be around. And you're so very good with her and once I'm back at work I won't be able to spend all my time with her.'

*Crash.* Jo's heart skidded straight off the track and into a barrier. He wanted her as a nanny.

*Well, of course, what else did you expect, you dreamy nitwit?*

She lifted her glass and took a gulp of wine. 'I'm sorry, Hugh,' she said, not quite looking into his face. 'I can't manage it. I've already got a good job in Brisbane.' Then, with a haughty tilt of her chin, she looked him squarely in the eyes. 'And I have a career plan. I've worked hard to get where I am. I'm afraid I can't just abandon everything here.'

He nodded thoughtfully, lifted his beer as if he was going to drink, and then set the glass down again. 'I'm sorry, I should have asked before this. What sort of work do you do?'

She hitched her chin a notch higher. 'I'm an accountant.'

He smiled. 'I'd never have picked you as an accountant. You seem too—'

'Too what?' she snapped.

His smile broadened to a grin. 'I was going to say relaxed.'

'So you're another one.'

'Another?'

'One of the millions who like to stereotype accountants.'

'Oh, touchy subject. My apologies.' Hugh lifted his beer again and this time he drank half of it quickly. As he set the glass down, he said, 'You're not accounting at the moment.'

'No,' she admitted. 'That's because I've taken my annual leave over the Christmas and New Year period, but I have to be back at work in a little over two weeks.'

Without hesitation, Hugh said, 'What about those two weeks? What are your plans for them?'

She was surprised by his persistence. 'I'm here to help Mum out with the shop—and to spend time with my family.'

Hugh nodded and his face grew serious.

Jo fiddled with the stem of her wineglass. She thought of what it would be like for Hugh on the long flight back to London with Ivy. How would he go about settling his little daughter into a big strange city like London?

Her natural inclination to be helpful kicked in.

'Do you have friends or family in London who can help you with Ivy?' she asked. 'What about a—a girlfriend?'

'My parents live in Devon. I have friends, of course, but—' He paused and sighed.

Jo waited…and an annoying anxiety twisted inside her.

'My girlfriend and I broke up recently,' he said at last.

Jo kept a very straight face.

'Actually, we broke up because of Ivy.'

'Really?' This time it was hard to hide her shock.

Hugh shrugged. 'No big deal. We were heading for the rocks anyway, but the crunch came when I found out that I had a daughter.'

'Perhaps if she met Ivy she might change her mind,' Jo suggested.

He shook his head. 'Not this woman. The point is that none of my friends would understand Ivy the way you do. It's not just that you have sisters her age. She's really taken to you and, besides, you understand what she's used to, and what she'll find strange about London.'

He was right, of course. She was sure Hugh could manage quite adequately without her, but she also knew she could be very useful. She could help to make the big transition smoother for Ivy.

'Do you have a boyfriend who'd object to your going away?' Hugh asked.

Jo gulped. ''Fraid not. I'm—um—between boyfriends at the moment.' There'd been no one else since Damien, but there was no need to mention that to Hugh.

Should she seriously consider his request? Should she do it for Ivy's sake? Could she go to London for just two weeks until Hugh found a really good nanny? 'How much would you pay me?' she asked.

She spluttered into her wineglass as he named a sum. 'For two weeks? That's out-and-out bribery.'

He smiled. 'I know.'

'What sort of transport business are you in?'

'Aeroplanes,' he said quickly, as if he wasn't eager to divulge details. 'There'll be no problem in getting you a seat on our flight.'

'I'll have to think about it.' Jo drained her wineglass and took a deep breath. She was determined not to be impulsive this time. She wasn't rushing anywhere simply because this charming Englishman had asked for her help.

Just the same, his offer was very tempting. If she tried to balance the pros and cons, there were so many pros... Two weeks in London...all that money...doing a good deed for Ivy's sake...

What about the cons? There had to be cons. She would be leaving her mother in the lurch, but Christmas was over. Besides, she deserved a bit of a holiday. What else? There had to be more reasons why she shouldn't go.

Hugh.

Hugh and his gorgeousness. Two weeks with him and she'd be head-over-heels in love with the man. Even though he would remain polite and simply treat her like a nice nanny, she would fall all the way in love and she'd come home an emotional wreck.

'Sorry, Hugh,' she said grimly. 'I'd like to help, but I can't. I really can't.'

He looked so disappointed she almost weakened.

So she jumped to her feet. 'What time will you call in the morning to pick up Ivy?'

'I'll collect her now,' he said crisply. 'There's no point in her spending any more time with you. She'd only get too attached.'


'What's the matter, love?' her mother asked as Jo returned to the house just before dusk. She'd taken a long walk by the creek after Hugh and Ivy had left and she'd shed a tear or three.

The silliest thing was that she'd been crying for Ivy as much as for Hugh. The thought of the two of them…

*Enough.* She had made her decision and it was time to forget about them. They were starting a new life together and she had to get on with *her* life.

'I'm just a little tired,' she said vaguely.

'Tired my foot,' scoffed Margie. Steam rose as she lifted the lid on a pot of vegetables boiling on the stove. 'You've done something silly, haven't you?'

'No, Mum.' Jo's voice developed an annoying squeak. 'I've been excessively sensible.'

'You've turned Hugh Strickland down.'

Jo gasped. 'How did you—?' She bit her lip hard. Turning away, she pulled out a chair and flopped into it and rested her elbows on the kitchen table. 'Yes,' she said. 'Hugh offered me money to help Ivy settle in London and I turned him down.'

Her mother replaced the lid on the saucepan and lowered the heat before taking a seat opposite Jo. 'You should have gone with him, Jo.'

'Of course I shouldn't. You need me here.'

'We'd manage without you.'

'Well, that's gratitude for you.'

'I'm grateful, love. You know that, but I'm sorry you didn't grab the chance to go with him. It would really make a difference for that little girl to have a friendly face among all those strangers in a foreign city.'

'I'm almost a stranger to her.'

'But already she's very fond of you.'

Jo sighed. 'Ivy will be fine, Mum. London's crawling with nice Aussie girls looking for work as nannies. Hugh will find one at the drop of a hat.'

Her mother's chest rose and fell as she released a long slow sigh. 'I thought you had more courage.'

'Courage? I'm not scared. What would I be scared of?'

'Hugh.'

A kind of strangled gasp broke from Jo. 'Don't be silly. He's a gentleman.'

'Of course he is. A very handsome and charming gentleman. That's why you're scared.'

'Mum!' Jo jumped to her feet. 'I don't want to talk about this. What would you know?'

'More than you could imagine,' Margie said quietly.

About to flounce out of the kitchen, Jo stopped. Her mother was looking...*different*...kind of wistful and sad...and Jo felt her heart begin a strange little wobble.

'There was a man, Jo—before your father.'

Jo was quite sure she didn't want to hear this.

'I've never forgotten him.'

Appalled, Jo wanted to leave, but was transfixed by the haunted regret in her mother's eyes.

'I was madly in love with him,' Margie said. 'And he wanted me to sail across the Pacific with him on a yacht.'

'Did you go?'

Her mother shook her head slowly. 'I wouldn't be telling you this story if I'd gone. I reckon I'd still be with him.'

A stab of pain pierced deep inside Jo. 'You don't know that. It mightn't have worked out.'

Her mother smiled sadly. 'Then again, it might have been wonderful. I'll never know.'

It was too awful to think of Margie Berry with another man. Jo thought of her mother's hard life—with an invalid husband and so many children.

'I don't regret my life,' her mother said. 'But I wish now that I'd gone. I might have been disappointed, but then...you never know.'

Margie had never given a hint that she wasn't happy, but the expression on her face now was like a window on another world. So many possibilities promised and lost...

Jo's throat was so tight she could hardly speak. 'But—but Hugh isn't asking me to go with *him*. He just wants a hand with Ivy.' She swallowed again. 'I'm not in love with him.'

'Pull the wool over someone else's eyes.' Margie stood and crossed the room and slipped her arm around her daughter's shoulders. 'I think you should go to London, Jo. You'll definitely be good for Ivy and, as for what else might happen, be brave, honey, and take the risk. At the very least it'll be a jolly sight more interesting than hanging around here for the rest of your holidays. And, believe me, you don't want to spend the rest of your life wondering what might have happened.'

The light was out in Hugh's hotel room when Jo gave a tentative knock at a little after eight. If he was already asleep she would slip away.

No chance.

The door opened quickly. And by the dim light of a fluorescent tube halfway down the veranda, she saw that he was shirtless, with a pair of unbuttoned jeans hanging loose around his hips, as if he'd just dragged them on.

'Hello, Jo.' His greeting was polite but lacking his usual warmth.

'Hi.' She swallowed and tried not to stare at his

rather splendid shoulders…or at the dark hair on his chest, trailing down… 'I'm sorry to disturb you.'

'I wasn't asleep.' He cocked his head back towards the darkened room. 'But Ivy is.' Stepping out on to the veranda, he closed the door gently. 'What did you want? Is anything the matter?'

'I—I wondered if it would be all right if I changed my mind—about coming to England.'

Hugh didn't answer straight away and he was standing close to the wall where his face was in shadow, so Jo was left hovering, filled with sudden doubts. Why on earth had she listened to her mother? This was crazy.

'I'd like to help you with Ivy,' she added.

'What made you change your mind?'

'I—I started thinking about her. She's had such a tough life, poor kid. I know everything's going to be fine for her now she has you, but if I can help you to smooth the way for her, right at the start—'

Again there was silence. Hugh's eagerness to have her help seemed to have vanished.

'Are you quite certain your family can spare you?'

'Yes, I've discussed it with Mum. She's actually keen for me to go.'

'Is she now?' For the first time, Hugh sounded faintly amused. 'Well, then.'

'Is—is your invitation still open?'

'It is,' he said at last.

Jo waited, feeling dreadful.

'So you're sure you'd like to come?'

'Yes.'

'You have a passport?'

'Yes, I do. I went to a conference in Singapore last year.'

'That's terrific,' he said and his smile was cautious as he extended his hand to shake hers.

That was all? A handshake?

Jo was horribly deflated as she walked home again—down the quiet main street, past the familiar, shabby little cluster of buildings that was her home town. The thought of swapping it for London had been so exciting. She'd been so worked up about reaching her decision and going to Hugh to tell him.

But somehow she'd kind of been expecting a little more enthusiasm from him. Another kiss perhaps…to continue what they'd started under the mistletoe.

Now she wondered if that had been the first and last kiss she'd ever share with Hugh. And an inner voice warned that trying to get close to Hugh Strickland would be dangerous.

In the middle of the street she stopped and she looked up at the vast star-speckled sky stretching overhead and she wished she'd stuck to her original decision.

Why on earth had she listened to her mother's fantasies about a might-have-been romance?

# CHAPTER FOUR

HUGH was worried. Not about Ivy—his first fears had been for her, but she was travelling like a veteran. However, there was something not quite right with Jo.

It wasn't her initial hesitation over coming to England that bothered him; she'd been happy enough when they'd left Bindi Creek and she'd laughed at her father when he'd warned her not to expect too much of England.

'England's a good place for the English,' he'd joked and she'd dismissed his gloomy cautions with a good-natured grin and an expressive roll of her eyes.

'Say what you like, Dad, you won't put me off. I'm going with an open mind.'

The change began in earnest when they reached Mascot Airport in Sydney and Jo realised that they weren't flying in a regular commercial jet.

'You're worried my plane won't keep you in the air?' Hugh suggested when he saw her pale face.

'No, it's not that. It's just that I've never known anyone who owned his own jet, let alone his own airline company. I hadn't realised you were quite so—so seriously wealthy.'

He'd expected to be interrogated. A straightforward girl like Jo would demand that he laid all his
cards on the table. But, to his surprise, she'd backed
right off.

She was subdued on the flight—although she was
wonderful with Ivy—reading to her, helping her with
a colouring-in book, being excessively patient when
Ivy insisted on colouring horses purple and chickens
bright blue. And, when Ivy had had enough, Jo found
a suitable movie from the video collection and she
made sure the little girl was perfectly comfortable
when it was time to sleep.

He'd thought that they might spend much of the
flight chatting, getting to know each other better,
even flirting a little, but Jo kept her distance. She
seemed determined to stick to her role as nanny and
nothing more—which was no doubt very sensible—
but it left Hugh feeling strangely dissatisfied.

She seemed happier when they finally landed at
Stanstead. They were met by Hugh's man,
Humphries. And, as they drove across London to
Chelsea, both Jo and Ivy peered from the car's windows with identical expressions of wide-eyed wonder. But when they turned into St Leonard's Terrace
and pulled up in front of his house, Jo looked worried
again.

'This is your new home,' she told Ivy. 'Isn't it
grand?'

'It's very tall,' Ivy said, dropping her head back
to look up. Then the little girl frowned as she viewed

the other houses up and down the street. 'Why are all the houses joined on to each other?'

Jo laughed. 'So they can fit lots of people into London.'

Ivy turned to Hugh. 'How many people can you fit into your house, Daddy?'

'Quite a few if I'm having a party, but most of the time there'll just be the three of us. And Humphries. Oh, and Regina, my housekeeper.'

'Do you have lots of parties?' Ivy asked, excited.

'Not these days.'

At one time there had been an interminable stream of parties, but now Hugh realised with something of a shock that he was looking forward to a quieter life, getting to know Ivy.

And Jo.

He noticed that Jo was shivering in her inadequate jacket. 'First thing tomorrow, we buy you and Ivy decent winter coats,' he said.

'Don't worry about me,' Jo protested. 'I won't be here long enough to make it worthwhile.'

Her gaze met his and then skittered away. She was definitely tense. It was almost as if she was deliberately distancing herself from him.

Regina greeted them with offers of cups of tea or supper, but neither Jo nor Ivy was hungry.

'You're tired,' Hugh said to Jo, noting her drawn pallor. 'Let me show you and Ivy to your rooms.' Everything should be ready here. He'd telephoned detailed instructions to Humphries and Regina.

'Yes, I want to see my room,' cried Ivy excitedly. 'Is it pretty?'

'I hope you'll like it. Come on, it's this way. You'll have to climb some stairs. Here, let me help you off with your jacket.'

As they mounted the stairs Ivy slipped her trusting little hand inside Hugh's and he experienced an unexpected flood of well-being. This was his little girl and he was bringing her home.

'Here we are,' he said when they reached the third floor.

The door to Ivy's room was standing ajar and at the first glimpse the little girl let out a delighted 'Wow!' Her eyes danced as she let go of Hugh's hand and crept on tiptoe across the carpet. 'It *is* pretty!' she whispered.

Regina had done a good job, Hugh decided, noting the new bedspread and matching curtains in a pale yellow, blue and rose floral print. A little student's desk and chair had been set near the window, complete with a box of pencils, note pads, a little pot of glue, a child's scissors and, on the floor beside the desk, a little cradle and—

'A baby doll!' Ivy fell to her knees and her eyes were huge as she stared in wonder. 'She's just like Tilly's.' She scooped up the doll. 'Oh, thank you, Daddy.' Then she was on her feet and hugging his legs. 'Thank you, thank you.'

Hugh blinked back the tears.

Beside him, Jo bent down and picked up the unicorn that had been abandoned in the excitement. 'Look, Howard,' she said, holding the fluffy toy near the doll. 'You have a little sister.'

'Yes,' giggled Ivy, taking Howard and embracing both toys. 'I'm their mummy.'

'Now for your room,' Hugh told Jo. 'There's a connecting door here, but you and Ivy have your own private *en suite* bathrooms. Is that OK?'

'Is that OK, Hugh?' Jo cried, giving him a strange look. 'Are you joking? Of course it's OK. You've seen my family's home.'

Remembering how nine Berrys shared one bath-room, Hugh felt his neck redden. He hurried ahead of her. 'Well, anyway, here's your room.'

Jo followed him slowly, looking about her with a serious, grim little half-smile. She dipped her head to smell the violets and rosebuds in the crystal vase on the dressing table and then she stepped up to the big double bed and traced the pale gold silk of the quilt with her fingertips and then the pillowcases and the pretty trim on the sheets.

'Snow-white sheets with drawn-thread cutwork and embroidery,' she said. 'I'm going to feel more like a princess than a nanny.'

There was a knock on the door and Humphries appeared. 'I have Miss Berry's suitcase.'

'Good man,' said Hugh. 'Bring it in, please.'

After Humphries had left again, Jo stood staring at her luggage sitting on the carpet at the end of her bed. 'I'm afraid my battered old suitcase looks rather dingy in the middle of such a lovely room.'

'You can stow it in a cupboard if it bothers you.'

'Yes.' She took a deep breath and squared her shoulders before looking at him and her intelligent brown eyes regarded him with shrewd wariness.

'What's the matter, Jo? Is there something not right?'

'Now I see where you come from, I can't believe you fitted in so well at Bindi Creek.'

'The differences are superficial,' he said. 'You'll fit in here too.'

Her face pulled into a disbelieving smile. 'We'll see.'

He was tempted—*very* tempted—to slip a comforting arm around her shoulders, but the look in Jo's eyes prompted him to slip his hands into his trouser pockets instead.

Jo crossed her arms over her chest and fixed him with her steady gaze. 'A girl can handle just so many surprises, Hugh. I think you and I need to sit down and have a serious talk.'

'Now?'

'No, we're all too tired now.'

Hugh was feeling more wired than tired, but he said, 'OK, I'll leave you to make yourself comfortable. My room's further along the hall.'

Her face broke into an unexpected grin. 'I bet the master bedroom is really something.'

His body reacted in an instant. 'You're welcome to come and take a look, if you like.'

'Oh, no,' she said quickly. Too quickly.

'It'd be a fair exchange, Jo,' he responded flippantly. 'You've shown me yours, so I'll show you mine.'

It was meant as a joke. No matter how much he'd like to have Jo in his bed, now wasn't the right moment. But, to his surprise, instead of accepting the joke and smiling, or telling him to drop dead, she looked upset and blushed brightly.

He felt a surge of dismay. What had happened to the light-hearted, level-headed Jo Berry? The sight of her blush bothered him and, damn it, *stirred* him, arousing the very desire he wanted to quench.

While he struggled to think of a way to lighten the moment, a plaintive cry came from Ivy's room.

'Jo, where are you?'

'I'm here,' Jo called.

The sound of a sob reached them and she quickly hurried back through the connecting door. Hugh followed.

Ivy had abandoned her toys and was huddled on the floor in the middle of her bedroom with tears running down her face. When she saw Hugh and Jo, she began to sob loudly and Hugh felt a panicky rush of alarm.

'What's the matter?' Jo said, dropping to her knees beside the weeping child.

'I don't know,' Ivy wailed. 'I got scared.'

'It's OK, you're just tired,' Jo said, hugging her. 'And everything here's a bit strange for you. What you need is to get into your pyjamas and then into your lovely bed. You'll feel better in the morning.'

'Would a cup of warm cocoa help?' asked Hugh, desperate to help.

Jo sent him a grateful smile. 'That would be lovely, wouldn't it, Ivy?'

His daughter gave her eyes a brave scrub and then nodded and Hugh dashed downstairs to the basement kitchen—a man on an urgent mission. By the time he returned, Jo had changed Ivy into a frilly white nightgown and the little girl's face looked pink and white and clean as if Jo had washed her as well.

Hugh held out the mug of cocoa.

'It's not too hot, is it?' asked Jo.

'I don't think so,' he said, but he wasn't sure. 'See what you think.'

He watched with interest as Jo tested the mug against her inner arm, then frowned and took a tiny sip. There were so many things to remember about caring for a child, especially this child who'd already experienced one horrendous accident. He wondered how many mistakes he would make. He felt again completely out of his depth.

'This is fine,' Jo said. 'Yummy, in fact.'

Ivy accepted the mug, drank deeply and beamed at him. 'It's very yummy, Daddy.' But she only drank half before her eyelids began to droop.

Jo was sitting on the edge of Ivy's bed and she

gently took the mug from her loosening grip and set it on the bedside table. Scant seconds later Ivy's head reached her pillow and she looked as if she'd fallen asleep.

Hugh began to tiptoe away. 'I'll just be—'

Ivy's eyes flashed open and Jo frowned at him and set a silencing finger against her lips. Chastened, he stood very still.

'Don't go away, Daddy,' Ivy demanded.

'Don't worry, Ivy. Daddy will stay right here till you're sound asleep,' Jo reassured her and Ivy's eyes closed again.

Somewhat gingerly, Hugh sat at the end of the bed. 'I'm here, poppet.'

With her eyes still closed, Ivy smiled and she looked so sweet and angelic he felt a surge of pride. Emotion lodged in his throat as a rock-hard lump. Good God, he was turning as hopelessly sentimental as his elderly Aunt Daphne.

And yet...

There was nothing sentimental about the way he felt when he looked at Jo.

As they sat together in the lamplit silence, Hugh let his mind play with the fantasy of helping Jo out of her clothes and into bed. He wondered what the chances were that the light tan on her arms and legs extended to her thighs and stomach...

'She's such a beautiful little girl.'

Jo's soft voice intruded into his pleasant musings.

Hugh smiled. 'I'm dreadfully biased, but I'm inclined to agree with you.'

'I'd say she's sound asleep now.'

But Jo didn't move and neither did Hugh. They continued to sit very still, super-conscious of each other's proximity as they watched Ivy.

'I imagine her mother must have been beautiful.'

'Linley? Yes, she was.' He sighed. 'But I'm afraid she was rather like a beautiful soap bubble or a butterfly. I felt as if I never got to the essence of her.'

'Oh.' Jo seemed to consider this as she watched Ivy thoughtfully. 'I don't think Ivy's like that.'

'No,' Hugh agreed. Even at the tender age of five, his daughter possessed an inner strength he'd never sensed in Linley.

Jo turned to him. She looked calmer now and she smiled sleepily.

'You look tired,' he murmured.

'Mmm. I am rather.' A wing of her hair fell across her cheek and she tucked it behind her ear.

In the past few days Hugh had seen her do this many times. He knew that before long her silky brown hair would slip forward again and he couldn't resist reaching out now to touch the soft curve of her exposed cheek. Her skin was as soft as a rosy-gold peach. 'Thanks for coming here, Jo.'

'I suppose I should be thanking you. I've never basked in so much luxury.'

'Treat this place like it's yours. Take whatever you like.'

She looked a little startled and Hugh couldn't resist leaning forward to drop a kiss on her surprised pink mouth. He heard the sharp intake of her breath and it sounded so sexy and her open lips were so warm and sweet that he kissed her again.

She had the loveliest mouth.

'Welcome to Britain, Jo Berry,' he murmured as he tested the soft, lush fullness of her lips.

'I'm very happy to be here,' came her breathless, throaty reply.

Hugh couldn't resist deepening the kiss and her lips drifted apart in open invitation. He reached for her hands and as he rose from the bed she came with him, moving slowly, languidly, almost floating, as in a dream. Next to the bed he drew her close and kissed her again and then he slipped his arm around her shoulders and she drifted beside him and he guided her to the doorway.

No sooner were they were out of Ivy's room and in the hallway than they fell into each other's arms and in a heartbeat their lips and tongues were sharing secrets they hadn't dared to speak of.

Hugh knew he was sinking fast. Jo was so sexy. She sounded and looked sexy and she tasted and felt incredibly sexy...

His hands explored the gorgeous curves of her bottom, the soft slenderness of her waist and then they found her breasts—beautifully full and soft and round—their tight peaks straining against the flimsy lace of her bra. With a soft, voluptuous moan she arched, pressing her breasts into his hands.

Rampant need inflamed him. He was losing control…

But then he realised Jo was pulling away from him.

She gasped, pressing her hands to her cheeks. 'This can't be real. I must be more jet lagged than I realised.'

*No.*

He was about to haul her back into his arms, to hurry her away with him to his bedroom, but her dark eyes looked directly into his and her gaze was intensely eloquent, as if she were pleading with him, commanding him to agree that their kiss had been a mistake.

Had it been a mistake? *Had it?*

His tormented body cried no!

But as Jo backed further away from him he knew that yes…it probably had been ill-advised.

Things could get very complicated if he dragged her to his bed the very minute he got her inside his front door.

'I'm going to follow Ivy's good example and get to sleep,' she said.

Hugh took a deep, still ragged breath. 'I'll ask Regina to bring a light supper on a tray to your room.'

'Thank you. Some cocoa and a sandwich would

be lovely.' Without looking his way again, she walked quickly away from him and into her room.

Next morning Jo and Ivy appeared in the dining room just as Hugh was helping himself to bacon and eggs. He'd spent a restless night—the combined result of jet lag and Jo.

But he was relieved to see that both Jo and Ivy were looking more chipper. Jo was looking exceptionally pretty, dressed in cream corduroy trousers and a soft wool sweater in a very fetching shade of deep pink. It seemed the perfect complement for her nut-brown hair and eyes.

She made Hugh think of…wild roses…on a summer's afternoon…

In fact, he found that he was staring.

'So that's what a full English breakfast looks like, is it?' she asked, eyeing his loaded plate.

He grinned, relieved that she seemed to take last night's incident in her stride. 'If you want the works you get sausages and baked beans as well. Of course, you don't have to have anything cooked.'

'Can I have some orange juice?' asked Ivy.

'Say please,' Jo reminded her.

'Please, Daddy?'

'Of course.'

'I'll just start with a cup of tea,' Jo said, helping herself to a cup and saucer as Hugh poured orange juice from a glass jug. 'I love this pink and white striped china. You have so many lovely things, Hugh.'

His mother had given him the china. At the time he'd thought it was a strange choice for a bachelor's pad, but whenever he'd brought young women home they'd adored it, and so he'd decided it was a definite asset.

Jo smiled when she lifted the teapot from the sideboard. 'Silver. I should have guessed.'

'Are you sure you wouldn't like something to eat?' he asked. 'Scrambled eggs or poached, or—?'

Behind him a door banged.

And a sharply elegant blonde, wearing an ankle-length silver fox fur coat, swept into the dining room. *Oh, God, no. Priscilla.*

Hugh had no chance to recover from the shock of seeing his former girlfriend before she flung herself at his neck.

'Darling, I heard you were back. I've missed you so-o-o-o much.'

Her arms latched around him and he was enveloped in fox fur as she pressed herself against him and kissed him on the mouth.

Stunned and angry, he struggled to extricate himself from her embrace. 'What are you doing here?' he gasped.

'What a silly question, Hugh, darling. I just had to be here to welcome you home.'

Hugh sent a quick glance in Jo's direction. She was looking as stunned as he felt. But Priscilla managed, very deftly, to ignore Jo. Her gaze—perfect blue, but crystal cold—flicked rapidly over her as if she didn't exist, before settling rather nervously on Ivy.

'And this is your little sweetheart,' she said, smiling a very forced, awkward smile.

Hugh glared at her. How could Priscilla do this? She'd broken up with him the minute she'd learned of Ivy's existence.

'You can't have us both,' she'd told him when she learned he was going to Australia to claim his daughter. 'Who will it be, Hugh—the child or me?'

'She's my flesh and blood,' he'd reminded her. 'My responsibility.'

'But you can't drag her into our lives now.' Priscilla had made his daughter sound like something the cat might bring back from a night's hunting. 'What would everyone think, Hugh? I'd be a joke!'

It was the last in a string of disappointments he'd experienced during their relationship. He'd had enough of Priscilla Mosley-Hart's tantrums and was more than glad to be rid of her.

He made no attempt to introduce Ivy, and so Priscilla bent forward stiffly, from the waist, and bared her teeth as she tried again, unsuccessfully, to smile at the child.

'What's your name, sweetheart?'

Ivy didn't answer.

Priscilla's plastic smile slipped, but she tried another tack. 'We'll be seeing a lot more of each other from now on, sweetheart.'

But Ivy had the good sense to remain silent and she watched Priscilla through narrowed eyes, as if she sensed she was in enemy territory.

'Oh, well,' said Priscilla with the air of someone who'd done her very best and couldn't be expected to succeed when a child was so obviously uncooperative.

Not for the first time, Hugh regretted the manners that had been hammered into him from birth. Unfortunate rules about the way a gentleman treated a lady prevented him from grabbing Priscilla by the scruff of her extravagant coat and marching her back through the front door.

He pressed a bell for Regina and his round-faced middle-aged housekeeper appeared at the door. 'Regina, would you mind taking Ivy to the kitchen and fixing her some breakfast?'

'I'd love to.' Regina beamed at Ivy. 'Come with me, ducks. Come and see all the lovely things I have for you. You must be so hungry after flying all the way from Australia.'

To Hugh's relief, Ivy seemed happy to escape downstairs.

'I'll go, too,' said Jo.

'No,' commanded Hugh sharply. Then, more gently, 'Please stay, Jo.' He wanted her to hear first-hand that his relationship with Priscilla was over.

'*I* think the nanny should leave,' Priscilla said with a sniff.

Hugh ignored her. Under no circumstances was she going to win this round. He said, 'Let me introduce Joanna.'

'Joanna?' Priscilla seemed to freeze and she turned to Jo with some difficulty.

Hugh took Jo by the elbow. 'This is Joanna Berry. She has come over from Australia and has very kindly—'

Priscilla let out an uncertain titter. 'What a sensible idea to bring an Australian nanny with you. She can do everything for Ivy before you find a school to send her to.'

How had he ever thought he was attracted to this woman? She was getting more ghastly by the minute.

Jo was standing very still with her eyes downcast, studying an antique table napkin. In one hand she held her cup and saucer, but she seemed to be paying great attention to the monogram on the napkin, running her fingertip over and over the embroidered initial R.

Priscilla gave a toss of her head. 'Now can we have some privacy, Hugh?'

'Why on earth do we want privacy?' Hugh injected a thread of menace into his voice—one Priscilla couldn't miss.

'What's the matter with you? That's a strange thing to ask your fiancée.'

'My *what*?'

Priscilla's smile was very brittle. 'Hugh, dear.' She lifted her left hand and pushed at a wing of her expensive hair and an enormous sapphire and diamond ring glinted on her fourth finger.

'Bloody hell, Priscilla, what game are you playing?'

Holding out her left hand, she waggled her fingers at him, making the sapphire and diamonds sparkle. She pouted. 'Our engagement is hardly a game, Hugh.'

'Our engagement? Have you gone mad? What's this ring?'

'I bought it at a sale at Sotheby's. Do you like it? It's just like the one we planned.'

'Like *hell*. We never planned any such thing.'

Beside him, Jo set down her cup and saucer and stepped away. 'I'm out of here,' she muttered, but Hugh moved quickly and reached for her arm and, at his touch, she froze.

Clearly put out, Priscilla fiddled with the ring, twisting it back and forth on her finger.

'Just tell me whatever it is you have to say, Priscilla.'

Ignoring Jo as best she could, she said, 'I know you want to forget my silly little outburst about dear little Ivy. I don't know what got into me. I was shocked. I was shaken. I wasn't thinking straight and it was all a mistake. Of course I didn't mean it when I said I wanted to break up.'

'I'm sorry, Priscilla,' Hugh said quietly, while he

held Jo's arm in a tight grip. 'It's too late to change your mind. You gave me an ultimatum. I was to choose between my daughter and you, and I made my choice.'

'But darling, I wasn't thinking straight. Of course you have to have your daughter with you.'

'Our relationship is over.'

'Like hell it is!'

'That's my final word.'

Priscilla gaped at him and then she pouted coyly like a spoilt little girl. 'But I'm planning to marry you, Hugh. Surely you always knew I would. I've booked the church.'

'Cancel it.'

A breathless silence filled the room. Hugh could feel white-hot anger sluicing through his veins.

Priscilla's eyes narrowed then and she directed a venomous glare at Jo, before swinging a blistering glance back to Hugh. 'This is *her* fault. She's got to you, hasn't she?'

'Stop right now.' Hugh spoke through gritted teeth. He'd known Priscilla had her imperfections, but he'd never seen this side of her before. Had she hidden it, or had he been blinded to it? 'Of course this isn't Jo's fault.'

He was surprised by the force of the rising anger surging through him and by his overpowering desire to protect Jo.

A kind of light-headed wildness overcame him and he slipped a possessive arm around Jo's shoulders.

The simple gesture had the desired effect. Priscilla sagged in horror as if she'd been kicked in the chest by a kung fu expert.

But she quickly rallied. Hatred flashed in her eyes. 'I can see she's got her nasty little claws into you already.'

'I'd advise you to shut up, Priscilla.'

She ignored him and directed her glare straight at Jo. 'You might be sleeping with him, but don't fool yourself that he would ever consider marrying you.'

Hugh felt a violent shudder pass through Jo and something inside him snapped. He had to defend her from this assault, even if it meant fighting dirty.

'That's exactly where you're wrong, Priscilla.' Hugh paused for dramatic effect.

Jo gasped.

And Priscilla screamed. 'You're not planning to marry *her*? You're mad. This is crazy. Your father will disinherit you.'

'Rubbish. He's delighted.'

'Now just hang on a minute,' interrupted Jo. Obviously embarrassed, she wrenched her arm out of Hugh's grasp. 'This is getting totally out of hand.' Outrage flashed in her eyes. 'I've had enough of listening to you two fight. I've more important things to do. I'm going to check on Ivy.'

With that she stormed out of the room—determined not to be involved in their little game.

Priscilla's lips curled into a sneer as she watched Jo leave. 'She might be a fast worker, but she's timid and flighty. She'll be the same as Linley Quartermaine. One thing's for sure, she won't last— not as your nanny—or as your fiancée.'

'It's time you left,' Hugh told her coldly. He should have chucked her out twenty minutes ago.

In desperation, Priscilla tried again to smile. 'You don't mean that, Hugh. I came here to tell you—'

'Leave right now, Priscilla. You've said more than is wise.'

She rolled her eyes. 'Don't you believe it; I've hardly begun.' And then, with a chilling, calculating smirk, she turned and sailed out of the opposite door from the one Jo had used.

Moments later Hugh heard the sharp click of her high heels in the marbled entry hall and shortly after that the front door slammed. And Jo came back upstairs.

She marched into the dining room, her face tense and tight and her hands planted on her hips, ready for battle.

'How's Ivy?' Hugh asked her quickly.

'She's fine—eating you out of house and home. I'll join her just as soon as we've had our little *chat*.'

'Jo, I'm sorry about that. Priscilla was abominable.'

'Yes, she was. But what are you up to, Hugh?'

He flinched.

Momentarily, her face crumpled. 'Why on earth did you let her think we're getting married?'

She looked so wretched a stab of pain pierced him in the chest.

To defend you and help me, he thought. 'To get through to her. To finish it,' he said.

'Surely you can wriggle out of a sticky situation with an old girlfriend without dragging me into it?'

'I know it was reckless of me, but at the time I was so furious with her.'

Jo glared at him. 'You didn't even deny that we're having sex.' She gave an accompanying stamp of her foot to show how very mad she was. 'You more or less said yeah, it's a red-hot relationship and we're going to get married.'

'That's not what I said at all.'

'It's what you implied.'

Hugh felt a surge of annoyance. He'd just had one woman take centre stage when he should have dropped the curtain on her. Now here was another!

He sighed. 'I was trying to defend you. I'm sorry.'

'It's a bit late for apologies. Priscilla's walked out of here convinced that we're having sex—which is dead wrong! And she thinks we're going to be married. Wrong again! What have you achieved? I can't see that you've done me any favours.'

Feeling cornered, he scratched the back of his neck. 'You have to admit, it was almost worth it to see the look on her face when she thought we were going to be married.'

Jo rolled her eyes to the ceiling, but a moment later a little smile tweaked the corner of her mouth.

'She did look like she'd been slapped in the face with a kipper.'

But then she gave an annoyed toss of her head. 'Don't try to sidetrack me, Hugh.' Eyeing him warily, she added, 'Just make sure you tell Priscilla the truth and tell her soon.'

The phone rang in the next room and he ignored it.

But Jo dived for the door. 'That might be Mum. I couldn't ring her last night because of the time difference, but she's expecting to hear if I've arrived here in one piece.'

She dashed to answer it, but she was back in less than a minute. 'It's your father,' she said, looking and sounding shaken.

*Bloody hell.*

'He's just congratulated me on my engagement to his only son. He was very polite and charming, but somehow I don't think he sounded too happy about it.'

Hugh groaned. The minute Priscilla had been out of the door she must have rung his father on her cellphone.

'You'd better sort it out, Hugh. I'm not prepared to continue this charade just so you can keep your Priscilla at arm's length.'

'Yes, you're right. I'll explain.'

The strange thing was, he thought as he headed to the phone, that for one reckless moment marrying Jo had seemed to make perfect sense.

# CHAPTER FIVE

WHAT a mess! What a dreadful, dreadful mistake she'd made by coming to England—to Chelsea—to this house, Hugh's house. She should never have listened to her mother.

As Hugh went to answer the phone, Jo was awash with tears. The door closed behind her with a gentle click and she stumbled across the room to put as much distance as possible between herself and Hugh's conversation with his father.

She felt terrible. She'd already been tired after the long flight and a long, restless night of tossing and turning as her mind wove fantasies about her and Hugh and now—*this*.

Priscilla was ghastly.

Of course she was rather beautiful in a plastic, ultra-expensive, super-model kind of way. And men fell for that sort of thing—but how could Hugh have ever liked her?

But then she knew nothing about him really. *Nothing*. Well, one thing. She knew that he had to be seriously wealthy—or seriously in debt. He apparently owned his own aviation company and this house was five storeys tall and in one of the swankiest parts of London.

But that was all she knew and there were so many questions screaming around inside her.

And the biggest question was how he could so casually claim to be marrying her. It made a complete mockery of her deepening feelings for him.

With an angry little huff, she looked out through the dining room window—actually, it was a pair of full-length French windows—and they opened on to a little balcony edged with a dainty wrought iron railing. Elegantly decorated porcelain pots on the balcony had been planted with carefully pruned topiary trees, each tree consisting of three neatly clipped balls.

Around each trunk a large red bow had been tied, presumably to provide a touch of Christmas. She wondered if they'd been Priscilla's idea.

Outside the house, the sky was winter white. Across the street there was a row of tall trees so bare that she could see right through the branches to a large playing field and a big, rather grand old building.

'That's the Royal Hospital.'

Hugh's voice sounded close behind her.

Jo's heart leapt as she swung around. 'I didn't hear you come in. That was a quick conversation.'

'Charles the Second had the hospital built for returned soldiers,' Hugh said. 'It was designed by Christopher Wren.'

Why was he suddenly talking about hospitals and history? 'What's the matter, Hugh?' He looked rather pale. 'Did you explain to your father that the engagement was all a mistake?'

He looked a little ashamed and awkward but, to her relief, he nodded.

'Thank heavens for that.'

'But I wasn't able to talk him out of coming up to London. He and Mother are coming up from Devon soon.'

'Well… I suppose they want to meet Ivy.'

Hugh sighed. 'Yes.' Turning back to the table, where his bacon and eggs still lay cold and untouched, he said, 'I've rather lost my appetite. Why don't I ask Regina to do something quick and easy—some fresh tea and hot buttered toast? Would that suit you?'

'Yes, of course, thank you.'

He disappeared and was back in a matter of minutes. 'Breakfast is on its way.'

'Hugh, before Regina and Ivy get here, *I'd* like to get a few things straight.'

Hugh flexed his shoulders, squared his jaw and then grinned at her.

Jo wasn't in a grinning mood, but his smile wrought its usual havoc on her heart. She tried to hide her distress behind a small smile. 'I think it's only fair that I know exactly who I'm dealing with while I'm working here,' she said.

'You're not working here, Jo. You're my guest.'

'If I'm not working, why did you offer me a great deal of money?'

Hugh didn't seem to have an answer.

'So,' Jo resumed, 'I'd appreciate it if you'd answer a few questions.'

'What would you like to know?'

'What school did you go to?'

He looked taken aback. 'Why do you need to know that?'

'*Please…* I'd just like to know.'

'OK, I went to Eton.'

'Right.' She'd been afraid that would be his answer. 'And that signet ring on your little finger. It has a crest that matches the one on the teapot and the teaspoons.'

'You're very observant.'

'Is it a family crest?'

He glanced idly at his little finger. 'Yes.'

Jo picked up a starched linen table napkin. 'What about this initial R? Is it significant?'

'Jo, you've missed your calling. You should drop accountancy and take up law. I feel like I'm being cross-examined.'

'And I feel like a mushroom.'

'A what?'

'Someone who's deliberately kept in the dark.'

With a helpless shrug, he said, 'The R stands for Rychester. My father, Felix Strickland, is the Earl of Rychester.'

*Oh, my God.*

Jo's face flamed as she thought of how well Hugh had seemed to fit in at Bindi Creek, eating a

Christmas dinner of cold salads on the veranda with her family, listening politely to her dad's corny jokes and her brothers' risqué campfire stories.

She gulped. 'Does that mean—it doesn't mean—you're not related to the Queen, are you?'

'Good heavens, no.'

'So, what are you called? Does an earl's son have a title?'

'In formal circles they stick a Lord in front of my name, but you don't have to worry about that.'

Oh, heavens. What had Lord Hugh Strickland really thought of her family?

She remembered the wistful, dreamy look on her mum's face when she'd urged her to go to London with Hugh. Poor Mum. If she'd been hoping for a romantic outcome from this venture, she was in for a major disappointment.

What a joke. What a disaster! How had Jo Berry from Bindi Creek entertained even the tiniest romantic fantasy about an involvement with an heir to a British earldom?

Far out! Her fledgling dream seemed so foolish now. She was such a child. 'I wish you'd told me, Hugh.'

'But I wasn't keeping it a secret. I just didn't see the need to make a big deal about my family. It's only a title.'

Taking a deep breath, she folded her arms across her chest. 'What about your parents? I bet they're not as low-key about all this as you are. I'm sure your father was very relieved to hear that you haven't rushed into an engagement with the hired help.'

Hugh gave an exasperated shake of his head. 'If it's any consolation, my father has never liked any girl I've introduced to him. Priscilla was at the top of his list of pet hates.'

Jo awarded Hugh's father a mental tick for his good taste. 'And, speaking of Priscilla, what about her? Does she have blue blood too?'

'Her father has a minor baronetcy.'

*Damn!* Somehow, Jo hadn't expected that. Silly of her, but she'd hoped to hear that Priscilla was *nouveau riche*—with a father who'd made all his money doing something that was generally frowned upon— like robbing banks or making pornographic movies.

But Priscilla was an aristocrat. All Hugh's circle were probably aristocrats—a club of exclusive peers of the realm. Jo's sense of alienation, her hurt and simmering anger, erupted. Tears threatened, stinging her eyes. 'I can't believe I let myself get into this mess.'

'Jo, don't be upset.'

'Why not? I have every right to be upset. Maybe it doesn't bother you that your old girlfriend is running all over London spreading the word that you're sleeping with your daughter's nanny—or worse, that you've got yourself engaged to a money-grubbing nobody from Australia.'

'I doubt Priscilla has the energy to stir up trouble.'

Jo didn't believe him. After four years working in

a city office, she'd witnessed enough broken affairs to know that a woman scorned had masses of energy and could cause all kinds of damage.

What a mess. If she wasn't very careful she would start crying, but she was too proud to break down in front of Hugh, so she squeezed her eyes tightly shut and took so many deep breaths she was in danger of hyperventilating.

'Jo, I really am very sorry to have caused you this distress.' Hugh's voice sounded worried. His hand touched her cheek.

Her eyes flew open.

His face was very close to hers and he was looking at her so tenderly she almost broke into very noisy sobbing. And then he gave her his endearing, crooked-sad smile. 'I can't bear to see you upset,' he said ever so gently. 'You're such a sunshiny girl. I want you to be happy here.'

She blinked—twice—and forced a watery smile. Hugh's gentle concern was breaking her heart. 'Don't worry about me,' she said, holding bravely on to her smile. 'I'm fine.'

'No, you're not.'

'Then I'll *be* fine, very soon.'

Hugh leant just a little closer and dropped a quick, warm kiss on her forehead. It was just a brotherly kiss, but it was very nice. Jo drew a deep breath. And then suddenly Hugh's hand was at her waist and he dropped another kiss on to her cheek.

A second kiss was *not* brotherly. A flash of awarencss zigzagged through her—and an unbearable longing for him to kiss her again.

But she knew she shouldn't let that happen. Not again. She should step away from him. Right now. Even if he wanted to, she mustn't let him kiss her the way he had last night. She mustn't submit. Hugh must realise how susceptible she was to his—

Oh, man. She'd hesitated too long.

His lips were already on hers. His hands were bracketing her face and he was taking a delicious sip at her top lip, and now, oh, *yes*, he was tasting her lower lip, drawing it gently between his teeth. And there was no way she could ask him to stop—especially when his hands shifted to her hips and, with a soft sound that was half a sigh, half a groan, he covered her mouth with his.

Her legs turned to liquid as he drew her against him. She could feel the hardness of his arousal and he began to kiss her with a thoroughness that stole her breath. His lips and tongue were hot and demanding—delving the soft, warm recesses of her mouth.

His hands slipped under her sweater to touch her bare waist and, just as it had last night, a wild longing broke loose inside her and he went on kissing her, as if he needed her desperately, as desperately as she needed him.

'Look what I found.'

A voice sounded in the doorway.

Breathless, stunned, they sprang apart. Jo's heart was going haywire.

Ivy came into the room with a huge fluffy marmalade cat in her arms. 'I found this pussy cat,' she said with a beaming smile.

Jo's head and heart were still spinning and she couldn't think of a thing to say. And then she felt a rush of shame. What must Ivy be thinking?

Hugh recovered first. 'Well, hello there.' His greeting sounded just a little breathless and he sent a quick sideways glance to Jo before he addressed his daughter. 'So you found Marmaduke?'

'Yes, I've been exploring and I found him under the stairs.'

'He's Humphries's cat, so be gentle with him.'

'And guess what else I found?'

Hugh glanced Jo's way again and he sent her a quick, worried smile. 'What else did you find?'

'Your Christmas tree, Daddy. Come and see, Jo, it's beautiful.'

'Hang on,' said Hugh. 'Here's Regina now with Jo's breakfast.'

As Hugh hurried to help his housekeeper with the heavily laden tray, Jo took a deep, steadying breath. The after-shock of Hugh's kiss seemed to reverberate all the way through her.

But thank heavens Ivy hadn't been upset by the sight of them pashing each other to oblivion.

Hugh looked particularly light-hearted as he joined her at the table. His eyes held Jo's for a shade longer than was necessary. Why? Was he flirting? She couldn't bear it if he was playing games with her.

She thought again of her mum and suddenly remembered her promise to phone her. 'Excuse me,' she said, jumping to her feet. 'I need to telephone home. Mum will be frantic.'

'By all means.'

'I'll be back in a minute.'

She supposed it must have been jet lag that hit her as she dialled her home phone number. She felt vague and disoriented and teary. But at least she managed to convince her mother that everything was absolutely fine and that she was very, very happy. However, she found the white lie exhausting and it was a relief to hang up.

Just as she did so, the phone rang again.

Jo started. Heavens, she was jittery. And then she stared at the phone, wondering if she should answer it. What if it was Priscilla, or Hugh's father?

She took a step back and looked through the doorway to the dining room. Hugh was busy showing Ivy how he liked to cut his toast and he paid no attention to the phone.

Her hand shook a little as she lifted the receiver. 'Hugh Strickland's residence,' she said and her voice came out squeaky and thin.

'Oh,' said a male voice. 'You must be Jo.'

'Yes, that's right.' She wondered nervously how this person knew about her. She thought of Priscilla and her stomach clenched.

'It's Rupert Eliot here,' the voice said. 'I'm a friend of Hugh's.'

He had a very nice voice, cultured and beautiful like Hugh's, and just as warm and friendly.

'Would you like to speak to Hugh?'

'No, that's not necessary. Hugh's coming to our party on New Year's Eve and Anne and I were hoping you could come too.'

He must have made a mistake. Surely he mustn't know she was the hired help. 'I'll—er—tell Hugh straight away,' she said.

'We're looking forward to meeting you, Jo,' Rupert added. 'Hugh rang me from Australia and said you were helping him with little Ivy. Make sure Hugh brings Ivy too. There'll be other children here and they'll be good playmates for her, so the sooner she gets to meet them the better.'

'That sounds lovely,' Jo said, feeling dazed. 'Thank you. Thank you very much.'

'We'll hope to see you on Friday then.'

Back in the dining room, as Hugh poured Jo a lovely hot cup of tea and plied her with toast, she told him of the phone call and he wasn't the least surprised.

'Rupert's my oldest and best friend,' he told her. 'His six-month-old daughter, Phoebe, is my goddaughter.'

She must have looked worried because Hugh rushed to reassure her. 'You'll really like Rupert.'

'He isn't a Lord or a Duke or anything, is he?'

Hugh grinned. 'He's an Honourable, but honestly you'd never know. He doesn't have a snobbish bone in his body.'

'He did sound rather nice on the phone.'

'Anne, his wife, is really wonderful. She's a mad keen gardener and just dotes on Phoebe.' Almost wistfully, he added, 'Rupert and Anne fell in love when they were both eighteen and they're as happy as pigs in mud.'

Jo decided she very much liked the sound of Rupert and Anne. But what on earth would she wear to their party?

Hugh, however, was one step ahead of her. He'd already made plans for a shopping expedition.

And later Jo decided she must have fallen under some kind of spell because, for the rest of the day, she had let Hugh lead her and Ivy to shops and exquisite boutiques all over Chelsea and Knightsbridge.

There had been a great deal of dashing about, jumping in and out of tall, sturdy, square-looking black taxi cabs, which Hugh had said was easier than taking his car and trying to find parking spaces.

The prices of the clothes were high enough to send Jo into credit cardiac arrest, but Hugh had taken complete charge of the purchasing and wouldn't listen to any of her protests.

By the time they'd arrived home, she and Ivy had an astonishing number of purchases, including beautiful winter coats for them both and a gorgeous, utterly *divine* red evening gown for Jo from a shop in Sloane Street.

'You'll need something glamorous to wear to the Eliots' party,' Hugh had insisted.

And, as she hadn't packed anything remotely formal, she'd had to agree.

Hugh had taken charge of the whole thing. He'd pointed the gown out to the assistant. 'I want Miss Berry to try that one. Take her away and if it fits and she likes it, we'll have it.'

'Would you like to see the young lady in the gown?' the assistant had asked.

'No,' he'd replied, sending Jo an unexpected wink and one of his bothersome smiles. 'Keep it as a surprise.'

There had been just one sticky moment when Ivy had spotted the toy department in Harrods and Hugh had been eager to rush in there and buy her the lot.

But just as he'd been about to dive inside, Jo had stopped him. 'I wonder if that's a good idea,' she'd said.

'Don't be a spoilsport, Jo.' She suspected that his look of stubborn resistance was one his own nanny must have endured on many occasions when he was a boy. 'It's not as if Ivy has a houseful of toys.'

'But already this week you've given her Howard and the baby doll and her beautiful new bedroom with all those school things and now an entire wardrobe of lovely clothes...'

'You think my money will spoil her?'

'If she gets too much too quickly.'

His eyes had twinkled as he smiled another charming smile. 'I've turned out OK, haven't I?'

Jo gave a roll of her eyes. No way would she comment on that. 'Ivy's not used to luxury.' As she said this, Jo had wondered if it was her own reaction she was talking about. It was hard not to feel uncomfortable about being surrounded by such wealth. It was such a far cry from home.

But then Hugh had let out an exaggerated, moody sigh and grinned. 'You're probably right. Women always know best.'

By then Ivy had already wandered right inside the toy department and she was entranced by a wind-up pig chugging across the floor.

'Can I have him, Daddy?' she'd asked as Hugh approached.

'Maybe not today, poppet.'

'But I want a pig!'

Hugh shot a here-we-go glance back to Jo. 'If you're very good I promise I'll buy you a pig another day,' he'd said as he reached down and scooped her up.

She'd begun to protest.

'It's time to go home to Howard and baby doll,' he'd said.

'And Marmaduke?' she'd asked, her eyes brightening quickly.

'And Marmaduke,' Hugh had agreed.

'Yes, let's go home. I love your home, Daddy.'

Hugh's eyes had gleamed with a suspicious sheen. 'It's your home too, poppet.'

As Jo slipped into her sumptuous bed that night, she was exhausted but almost too excited to sleep. A whole day with Hugh had been intoxicating. He'd been so much fun, so generous, so solicitous, and so full of compliments, both for her and for Ivy.

She knew that the inevitable was happening; she couldn't help herself. Even though she'd started out by trying to resist Hugh, she was falling way past head over heels and into the deepest depths of being hopelessly in love with the man.

And all the time they'd been shopping—when she'd been under his spell—and remembering his kisses—a romantic future beyond the brief two weeks had almost—*almost*—seemed possible.

The problem was that now, as she lay alone in the dark, listening to the muffled sound of distant traffic on the King's Road, the happiness of her day with Hugh seemed unreal.

Of course she would be going back to Australia at the end of the two weeks. Hugh had his little daughter. He and Ivy were wrapped up in each other.

They didn't really need Jo at all.

# CHAPTER SIX

'DADDY?'

Ivy's voice came through the darkness just as Hugh passed her room.

Her door was halfway open and he gently pushed it further. 'Did you want something, poppet?'

'Can you tuck me in?'

'Yes, if you like.'

A newly purchased night-light in the shape of a toadstool stood on Ivy's bedside table, casting a warm pink glow across her bed, making her look rosy and prettier than ever, and Hugh felt a swift clutch of emotion.

'You look rather nicely tucked in to me,' he said, eyeing her neat bedclothes. 'What would you like me to do?'

'Daddy,' Ivy scolded. 'Tucking me in doesn't just mean tucking me in.'

'It doesn't? What does it mean then?' He felt lost again for a moment.

Ivy's bottom lip stuck out and her dark brows drew down into a stubborn frown. 'You should know.'

'Should I?' He swallowed a constriction in his throat. For the life of him he couldn't ever remember his own father tucking him into bed when he was a youngster. His mother had…but mothers and nannies were different, weren't they…and he'd been sent away to school when he was quite young. 'I'm sorry, Ivy. I've never had a little girl before.'

She turned her head to the side and looked towards the door that led to Jo's room. 'Jo knows what to do.'

'Well, yes.' Hugh sighed. 'That's because—because she has little sisters.' As Ivy continued to look sulky, he said, 'I'd love to tuck you in properly, sweetheart.'

'Don't call me that word.'

'Sweetheart? Why not?'

'That's what *she* calls me.'

'Who? Jo?'

'No. Gorilla.'

*Gorilla?* She meant Priscilla, of course. Hugh had difficulty suppressing his smile.

'I promise never to call you the S word again,' he said solemnly. 'Now, tell me what Jo does when she tucks you in.'

Ivy patted the bed. 'She sits here.'

'Oh, yes, of course,' said Hugh, lowering himself on to the edge of the bed.

'And she tells me a story, but you don't have to tell me a story.'

That was a relief. Hugh knew he wasn't much of a story-teller.

He watched Ivy looking up at him with trusting

expectation and he realised with a rush of happiness that there was no need to ask her what Jo did next. 'I've just worked out what a daddy should do now,' he said.

'What?' she asked, her green eyes sparkling suddenly.

Hugh picked up her hand. 'I should eat you up, starting at the fingertips.' He growled playfully as he began to nibble.

'No,' Ivy squealed, delighted.

'No? Then I should tickle you,' he suggested, tickling her ribs.

'No, no,' she protested amidst a flood of giggles.

'Have I still got it wrong?' He gave a deep, exaggerated sigh. 'Then, there's nothing for it, I'll just have to cuddle you and kiss you goodnight.'

'Yes!' With an excited cry she held out her arms. And Hugh gathered her up.

His heart swelled. She was his little girl. His very own. She felt so tiny and warm and she smelled of clean nightgown and the delicately scented special soap Jo used to bathe her sensitive skin. And she clung to him, her little heart beating against his. He kissed her cheek.

'I love you, Daddy.'

'I love you too, poppet.'

He hugged her again and then released her and she sank happily back on to her pillow.

'I like that name.'

'Poppet?'

'Yes.'

'Good. I like it too. It's my special name for you.' He kissed her forehead.

'I'm so glad you came and founded me. Ellen told me you would come and I've been waiting for you for so-o-o long.'

Hugh's heart ached for her. 'I'm glad I found you too. Now, goodnight, sleep tight.'

'I will.'

Ivy reached for Howard and closed her eyes and Hugh's throat tightened with a welling of emotion, stronger than anything he'd thought possible. He was astonished and deeply moved by how quickly and completely his little girl had opened her heart to him.

As he watched her, she hugged the unicorn closer and the sleeve of her nightgown bunched, revealing the terrible burn scars on her arm, and he felt a sharp, savage twist to his heart, so intense that he thought he might actually cry. Fearful that Ivy might open her eyes and see his distress, he turned and walked quickly to his own room. What fierce, sweet agony it was to be a father. He wondered if he was adequate for the task.

He slumped on to the side of his bed and began to unbutton his shirt, lost in thought. So much tragedy had clouded his daughter's early life.

And yet in spite of that she was such a lively, spirited, loving little thing. But she had big battles ahead of her.

No matter how carefully he chose her school there

would be inevitable taunts about her burned skin from some of the children. And in the future, as she grew, she would have to face more trips to hospital and more painful skin grafts.

If Ivy was going to remain lively and spirited and grow into a happy, well-adjusted adult, she needed strong, positive, loving forces in her life.

Was he man enough for the task?

Until very recently he'd been a rather selfish man, but now he had little choice; he had to change. As his father had been telling him for years, he had to take life more seriously. The thing was, he found running a business and making money relatively easy. Personal relationships were more problematical.

His friendship with Rupert and Anne Eliot had been one of his sounder personal choices. His selection of women, on the other hand, had been lots of fun but less prudent. His girlfriends usually proved to be more decorative than reliable.

Priscilla was a prime example.

*Damn.*

The shoe he'd just removed fell to the floor with a thud as he remembered. He'd promised Jo he would phone Priscilla and set the record straight. But he'd had so much fun taking Jo and Ivy shopping today he'd forgotten.

He would have to plan his speech very carefully before he rang. It was important to hit exactly the right note and it wasn't going to be easy. First he had to squash Priscilla's assumption that he'd been sleeping with Jo; and then he had to confess that he'd lied about asking Jo to marry him; and finally he needed to block any opportunity for Priscilla to belittle Jo in any way.

Rather a tall order—especially when he also had to ensure that Priscilla was left in no doubt that he wanted her out of his life—and he most definitely didn't want her anywhere near his daughter.

It was mid-afternoon the next day before he made the call. He was at his office in the city, where he'd been attending to urgent business that couldn't be left until after the New Year weekend. But his guilty conscience was nagging him and at last he punched Priscilla's speed dial number into his cellphone.

She recognised his number even before he spoke. 'Hello, Hugh,' she purred. 'What a delightful surprise. What can I do for you, darling?'

He thought he'd prepared for this call, but suddenly his concentration—super-focused when dealing with business matters—was distracted by a kind of sixth sense, a vague feeling of unease, a suspicion aroused by the fact that Priscilla sounded far too relaxed and happy.

Was she plotting something?

'Darling?' Priscilla's voice repeated.

She'd never called him darling when they'd been a couple, and the hollow meaninglessness of the endearment set his teeth on edge now. 'Good afternoon, Gorilla, I hope you're feeling calmer today.'

'I beg your pardon?'

'I said I hope you're feeling—'

'Not that. What did you call me?'

'I don't know. I called you Priscilla, didn't I?'

'It sounded like Gorilla.'

Had he really made that slip? 'Good God, no,' he protested. 'Impossible. So, how are you?'

'Calm as a millpond. We're having an absolutely fab time—afternoon tea at The Ritz.'

'How nice.' It had been raining heavily since lunch time and taking tea in one of the city's grand hotels while the rain fell on others less fortunate outside was a predictable, Priscilla-style activity.

He could picture her adopting her Marie Antoinette pose as she lifted a crystal champagne flute or a teacup—azure blue with a thick gold rim— or took a leisurely nibble at a dainty cucumber and smoked salmon sandwich. Yes, she *would* be at The Ritz; he could even hear a string trio playing Mozart in the background.

Somewhat reassured that she was out of harm's way, Hugh refocused his attention on his line of attack.

'You'll never guess who's here with me,' she said.

Distracted, it took a moment or two for her question to register. 'Oh?'

'Jo and Ivy.'

*'What?'* Fine hairs rose on the back of Hugh's

neck. His gut clenched as he leapt from his swivel chair. Jo and Ivy had gone sightseeing today.

Priscilla chuckled. 'Isn't it a lucky coincidence?'

*Like hell it was.*

'I ran into the poor things just as they were leaving Hyde Park.'

It was more likely that she'd been stalking them.

'Hugh, you should tell your international visitors never to go out in London without an umbrella. The poor darlings were absolutely drenched and it was freezing cold. Poor little Ivy could have caught pneumonia. Of course I insisted on giving them a lift to The Ritz to dry off.'

By now Hugh had grabbed his coat and was shrugging his shoulders into it as he clutched his cellphone to his ear. 'How are they?' he barked as he rushed out of the office.

'They're absolutely peachy *now*, darling. Jo's enjoying a cup of Earl Grey and Ivy's stuffing herself with scones and strawberry jam and cream.'

Hugh knew this pretence at cosiness was nonsense. There was no way Priscilla would make such an about-turn without a reason. A rotten, sneaky reason.

He was absolutely certain she hadn't extended such a conciliatory gesture to Jo out of the goodness of her heart. As the lift shot him to the car park in the basement, he tried to think of a way to keep the conversation going. He needed to distract Priscilla from whatever she had planned.

But, just as he reached his car, Priscilla said, 'Oh,

sorry, Hugh. We have an emergency. Ivy needs to go to the ladies' room.' And she hung up.

He considered calling straight back again, but chances were she wouldn't answer and he decided instead to concentrate on his driving. He needed to make his way through the rain and the traffic as quickly as possible.

He felt ill with dread as he steered his car through driving sheets of rain, but as he turned down Piccadilly, he tried to convince himself his fears were illogical.

Priscilla might have turned nasty, but she wasn't evil. And what could happen to Jo or Ivy at The Ritz? The place was swarming with staff trained to watch over their patrons and to attend to their every whim.

Swerving into Arlington Street, his tyres sent up a spray of rainwater and another shower as he came to a halt quite close to The Ritz's commissionaire. But the good fellow, dressed in his greatcoat and top hat and armed with a huge black umbrella, greeted him with his customary courteous smile.

'Would you like us to park your car, Lord Strickland?'

'Thanks,' Hugh muttered, tossing the keys to him. He had no time for their usual exchange of pleasantries as he dashed through the rain to the huge revolving doors.

Where were Jo and Ivy?

His gaze darted everywhere as he strode through the spacious lobby. He had no idea if Priscilla was here or in The Ritz's famous Palm Court restaurant. Most people needed to make a reservation for afternoon tea in the Palm Court and Priscilla might have done so but, then again, she was a notorious queue jumper.

One thing was certain; when Hugh found her, he was going to make sure that the first message she got was to get the hell out of his life. He wasn't prepared to have her anywhere near his daughter—or Jo!

And then suddenly he saw Priscilla, walking through the lobby, looking about her in much the same manner as he was. Alone.

Surprised to see him, she blinked. 'Hugh, what are you doing here?'

'I came to have a word with you.'

Something in his tone must have alerted her. She looked suddenly wary. 'Hold it, Hugh. Don't say a thing you might regret. The most important thing right now is to find your daughter.'

'What?' Hugh felt as if he'd been slugged. 'What the hell do you mean?'

'The poor little sweetheart. I'm trying not to think the worst, but dear little Ivy has disappeared.'

'How could she?' Hugh roared so loudly that several heads turned their way. 'What have you done?' He couldn't bear this. He grabbed Priscilla's arm. 'Where's Jo?'

'Who knows where Jo is? She panicked and took off. She's no good in a crisis.'

That was rubbish but he didn't have time to argue. 'Where was Ivy when you last saw her?'

Priscilla shrugged. 'She went to the ladies' room and didn't come back.'

'Where? Which ladies' room? Have you searched every cubicle?'

She slipped her arm through his and snuggled against him. 'Come with me, darling. I'll do my best to show you where she was last seen.'

Hugh shook her off. 'Just lead the way and be quick about it.'

As they rounded a corner Jo came towards them. And, in spite of Hugh's terror, he felt an immediate lift in his heart. But, to his surprise, she was walking at a sedate pace and she didn't seem particularly distressed.

'Have you found Ivy?' he demanded. But it was a foolish question. Surely if she'd found the child she wouldn't be alone.

'Not yet,' she said calmly. 'But I'm sure she'll turn up soon.'

Her composure annoyed him. 'How can you be so sure? Have you alerted the staff?'

'Yes, and I'm sure they'll find her. She must have gone exploring.'

'What about the police?'

'The police, Hugh?' Her brown eyes rounded with surprise. 'No. I didn't want to overreact.'

Hugh ploughed frantic hands through his hair. 'I can't believe this.' He reached for his cellphone.

'What are you doing?'

'Calling the police, of course.'

Jo laid a restraining hand on his arm. 'Just a minute, Hugh. Calm down. Ivy has been missing for ten minutes. Isn't it a bit early to call the police? We don't want to make a fuss about nothing. I'm sure she'll turn up any minute now.'

What had happened to warm, caring Jo? 'How can you be so damn casual?'

'This is a big hotel and a little girl has wandered off,' she said. 'But, for goodness' sake, the place is full of very nice, charming people, who will be only too happy to help her to find us.'

Her forehead creased as she peered at him more intently. 'Do you really think London is a mass of kidnappers just waiting to jump on her?'

*Yes*, he wanted to shout. A part of him knew he was overreacting but he just didn't know what a father should do in a situation like this.

But, at that very moment, Jo glanced past his shoulder and smiled. 'Look, just as I thought. Here she is.'

Hugh spun around and a desperate, choking little laugh broke from him. There was Ivy walking along the corridor, holding hands and chatting happily with an elegantly dressed, sweetly smiling elderly lady.

The moment she saw him, Ivy let go of the woman's hand and rushed forward excitedly.

'Daddy!' She hurled herself at his waist. 'What are you doing here?'

Hugh was so overcome, so suddenly confused, he couldn't speak. He simply patted Ivy's head while she clung to him and, although his heart was galloping like a steeplechaser, he noted that her hair was only a little damp and her clothes weren't wet at all. Obviously Priscilla's claim that she'd been drenched was an exaggeration.

He heard Jo thanking the elderly woman profusely and he took a deep breath and blinked several times to try to clear his eyes.

Jo knelt in front of Ivy. 'Where were you? We've been searching everywhere. You gave Daddy a terrible fright.'

Ivy gave a puzzled shrug. 'Gorilla took me to see the big Christmas tree and told me to hide there. She said it was a game and I had to wait there for you to find me, Jo. But you didn't come.'

'That scheming—' Hugh spun around, looking for Priscilla, and realised that Jo was doing the same.

'Where is she?' they both asked simultaneously.

But it was rather obvious that she'd taken off.

Jo's lip curled into a very un-Jo-like malicious sneer. 'She plotted this.' She shook her head in disbelief. 'She was trying to make me look bad—trying to prove that I don't know how to look after Ivy.'

'I can't believe you got in the car with her.'

Jo sighed. 'She made me feel terribly guilty about having Ivy out in the rain. But Ivy's coat has a hood. She was fine, really.' She darted Hugh a shrewd glance. 'How did you get here so fast? Did Priscilla phone you?'

'No,' he said. 'As a matter of fact *I* was ringing *her* to—' He broke off, not keen to admit that he still hadn't carried out his promise to set Priscilla straight.

With one arm around Ivy, holding her close, he watched the play of emotions on Jo's expressive face as she stood regarding him with her arms wrapped over her middle.

'You haven't spoken to her yet, have you?'

'I was about to.' He knew that was the lamest excuse under the sun.

'No wonder she tried to quiz me. She still doesn't know, does she? It's your job to set her straight, Hugh, not mine.'

'I'm sorry.' He chanced a smile. Jo was looking very fetching in an ivory-cream sweater, tweed skirt and knee-high brown leather boots that he'd bought her in Knightsbridge yesterday. 'What did you tell her?'

'Oh, what does it matter?' she cried angrily. 'I should never have spoken to her. I shouldn't have let her persuade me to come here with her.'

He stepped towards her and reached out to pat her shoulder, but she jerked away quickly and sent him a sharp hands-off look.

He had to hand it to Priscilla. She'd managed to upset everyone.

'I'll take you home,' he said.

'Goody.' Ivy beamed.

Jo merely nodded. And then, 'I'll fetch our coats.'

As they approached the heavy revolving doors, Jo took Ivy's hand and Hugh let them go ahead. Through the glass, he could see a policeman on the footpath, talking to someone. And then, as the door rotated and he stepped into the next available space, Jo and Ivy reached outside.

Hugh shoved at the door and pushed his way forward.

The policeman turned. 'Lord Strickland?'

'Yes?' Hugh snapped. 'What do you want?'

'We've received a report that your little daughter is missing.'

*Damn.*

# CHAPTER SEVEN

JO WOKE to the shrill ringing of a telephone.

She lay in the semi-paralysed state of the still-half-asleep and it seemed to take ages for her mind to kick into gear. When it did, she remembered that she'd been dreaming about phone calls…lots of phone calls… *weird* calls…from home, from Priscilla, from her boss in Brisbane, even one bizarre call from Queen Elizabeth the Second.

As she pushed her bedclothes aside and swung her feet over the edge of the bed, the phone downstairs rang again, and she wondered if it had been ringing a lot this morning. Perhaps it was the sound of many phone calls that had penetrated her sleep and prompted her strange dreams.

Had something happened? Some kind of emergency?

Her mind flashed back to last night. Hugh had been moody and distracted, but he hadn't wanted to talk about it with her. In fact he'd gone out.

Ivy had been dog-tired and had fallen asleep quite early, but Jo hadn't been able to sleep till after midnight. She hadn't heard Hugh come home.

Again the phone rang. What was going on? Her

feet sank into the deep pile carpet as she hurried to check on Ivy. She was gone.

Her first reaction was to panic, but then she told herself that was silly. Nevertheless, she washed her face quickly and dressed in haste, paying no more attention to her hair than to drag a quick brush through it before she rushed downstairs.

And, of course, there had been no need to panic.

Ivy was at the dining table, still in her pyjamas and with her hair a mass of sleep-tousled curls, and Hugh was helping her to take the top off a boiled egg that sat in a bright red hen-shaped eggcup.

He offered Jo a rather grim smile as she hurried into the room. 'Good morning.'

Ivy waved a gleeful spoon at her. 'We started breakfast without you.'

'Sorry, I slept in.'

'That's no mean feat, considering all the phone calls,' said Hugh.

So she'd been right. There had been a lot of calls even before she had woken. 'Why so many? What's happened?'

Hugh shrugged as if to make light of her query, but then his face twisted into an angry scowl. 'Have a cup of tea before you try to face the day.'

'What does that mean?' she asked as she lifted the silver teapot.

He didn't answer, but his scowl remained stiffly in place as he watched Ivy dip a finger of toast into her softly boiled egg.

'Come on, Hugh, tell me what's happened.' The worried tension in his eyes frightened Jo. 'Does it involve me?'

'I'm afraid so.' His glance shifted to a folded newspaper lying on the dining table.

Jo's teacup rattled against its saucer and she set it down quickly. She felt ill. 'Don't tell me there's a story in the paper. Priscilla hasn't run to the press?'

'Don't worry, it's a load of nonsense. And this is a discredited rag. No one takes any notice of it.'

'If no one takes any notice, why have there been so many phone calls?'

Even as she spoke, the phone rang again in the next room. She glanced expectantly at Hugh. 'Are you letting the answering machine deal with them?'

'Humphries is handling all the calls,' he said. 'He's doing a sterling job, diverting press enquiries to my PR fellow and vetting the private messages. I'll deal with those later.'

Jo's gaze flashed back to the newspaper—a potential time bomb just sitting there on the table—looking innocuous in the middle of all the breakfast things.

Hugh leaned closer to Ivy. 'Poppet, how would you like to have breakfast down in the kitchen with Regina again?'

She grinned. 'And Marmaduke?'

'Yes, Marmaduke will be there too.'

'Can I take my egg?'

'Of course.'

'Is Jo coming?'

'No, Jo and I need to talk about something.'

Hugh's ominous tone caused a lead weight to settle in the pit of Jo's stomach. She reached for the paper as soon as he and Ivy left the room, but she didn't want to read whatever was printed there.

And yet, if it involved her...and if the entire London populace already knew what it said...she had to face the worst.

The paper shook in her hands as she unfolded it and scanned the headlines. At first she couldn't see anything except general news stories. But then she saw a column—*Nelson's Column*—down the left-hand side and Hugh's name jumped out at her.

Sinking into a chair, she began to read.

*The Lord's Love-Child*

*Publicity-shy and supposedly squeaky-clean Lord Hugh Strickland, only son of the Earl of Rychester, has finally blotted the family's impeccable copybook.*

*Not one to do things by halves, the charming Lord Hugh is now at the centre of a growing scandal featuring the suicide of an abandoned lover and the sudden appearance of an illegitimate child, flown from Australia earlier this week.*

*Obviously the powerful and influential family went to great lengths to keep this a dark secret, particularly the fact that Strickland's love-child, a sick and delicate little girl, has a severe deformity.*

No! Oh, God, no! Dropping the paper, Jo covered her face with her hands. How could they say something so terrible about Ivy? This was much worse than she'd feared. She wasn't sure she could bear it.

Could it get any worse?

Sick with dread, she forced herself to read on…

*And it could have remained a family secret but for the bungling of an unqualified Aussie nanny who lost the child on her first outing in London yesterday.*

*A lost child sparks a call to the police, which in turn alerts the media (to keep you fully informed of the scandalous facts, dear reader)…and, as usual, this column is delighted to provide a vital link in the info chain.*

*How does a nanny lose a child on a visit to one of London's grandest hotels?*

*Perhaps it's not surprising when the attractive but totally disoriented nanny only has eyes for Lord Hugh…*

*The nanny, one Jo Berry, has no training or qualifications for the task (her previous experience has been with cattle, sheep and wombats) but apparently she's the hottest thing that the dashing Lord set eyes on when he made a mysterious visit to the wilds of the Australian outback recently.*

*It is obvious that the relationship is much more than nanny to Strickland's love-child and a source close to the family reports that an engagement has been announced to shocked family and friends.*

*But perhaps we shouldn't be too harsh on poor Miss Bindi Creek (Yes, dear readers, there is such a place, I assure you).*

*It's no wonder she forgot she was guarding a defenceless little girl whose medical condition requires constant attention.*

*Jo Berry probably had stars in her eyes, visions of diamond rings, a society wedding and a honeymoon spent rolling naked in the Rychester estate money.*

*But here's some free advice for little Miss Bindi Creek:*

*'You can lose the diamonds, darling, or even the engraved family silver...but not the daughter of the heir to the estate of the Earl of Rychester.'*

*The fiery old Earl himself is about to intervene and even this intrepid reporter wouldn't want to be around when that happens!*

*So, readers, stand by for official denials about any impending marriage and watch for the imminent return of Miss Bindi Creek to her distant native soil.*

Jo thought she might throw up.

Each sentence was like a knife thrust. She couldn't bear it. She'd heard of gutter press but she'd never imagined such awful journalism was possible. There were so many lies. Every word was a lie.

Unable to bear the sight of that ghastly print, she

closed her eyes, but from beneath her lids tears spilled down her cheeks. Hurt and indignation welled in her throat.

'Jo, it's a beat-up column by a broken-down hack.'

Hugh's voice startled her. She hadn't heard him return.

Looking up, she slapped at the newspaper in her lap. 'This is Priscilla's work, isn't it? This is all because of that stupid smokescreen engagement.'

'Yes,' he admitted. 'I didn't expect her to be so quick off the mark—or so vicious.'

Tears blinded her. She was trembling with anger and outrage.

'Jo, I promise you, I've dealt with Priscilla now. Last night. She won't cause you any more problems.'

*'She doesn't need to!* She's already done her worst.' With an angry yelp, Jo tossed the paper on to the floor and stomped on it. 'How can any journalist write such filth? Everything in it's a lie. They're all vicious lies. It's totally, totally despicable. One hundred per cent wrong. It's vile.'

Pressing her fingers against her lips, she tried to stop her mouth from twisting out of shape.

But she couldn't stop herself from crying. She felt violated. Betrayed.

Hugh reached for her and she tried to bat him away, but he drew her close and she was too overcome, too helpless to hold back. Her head fell on to his strong, bulky shoulder and she clung to him as she sobbed her heart out.

'I'm sorry, Jo,' he said in a husky whisper. 'I'm really sorry that this has happened.'

She wanted to be mad at him. She *was* mad at him. But he sounded so genuinely sorry that she found herself forgiving him.

And, as her sobbing slowed, she realised that it was rather comforting to nestle into his reassuring strength, to feel his protective hand stroking her head. He was actually being rather patient with her. He wasn't annoyed by her tears as many men might be. He held her as if he had all the time in the world.

He held her as if he cared. Really cared. And that made such a difference.

When at last she felt calmer, she lifted her head. 'This must be awful for you too, Hugh.'

But all he said was, 'I'm furious and incensed for you and for Ivy.'

She stepped away from him and her eyes searched his face, trying to read his true feelings beneath the calm, handsome façade. 'I guess this is what people with high profiles have to put up with.'

'Yes, it goes with the territory. But don't worry, this will backfire on Priscilla. She'll be *persona non grata* among our friends.'

There was a careful knock on the door behind them.

Hugh turned. 'Yes, what is it?'

Humphries took two steps into the room. 'I have a message from the QC you asked me to contact.'

'Good man, what did she say?'

'She's afraid that a successful action is unlikely, sir—and going to trial would be very messy and distressing.'

'I see.' Hugh's green eyes were thoughtful as he stood with his hands on his hips. 'I can't say I'm really surprised.'

'Why not?' Jo couldn't help asking. 'There isn't a grain of truth in that column. Surely you can sue them? The whole thing's a stack of garbage.'

'Yes, it's a stack of garbage, but unfortunately it's garbage piled on top of some basic facts.'

'Facts?' she cried. 'There's nothing factual.'

'Thank you, Humphries,' Hugh said and, with a courteous bow of his head, Humphries left them.

Hugh turned back to Jo. 'I'm afraid we're just going to have to ride this out. There's no point in getting tangled up in a long and drawn out court case and having the media stirred into a frenzy.'

Jo frowned. 'What did you mean before—about facts? Where were the facts?'

Letting out his breath slowly, he leant a hip against the table and folded his arms over his chest. 'Well, there's Linley's suicide...'

'OK,' she said slowly. 'That might be true, but I didn't lose Ivy yesterday. And to say that Ivy is deformed! That's a terrible thing to say about such a beautiful little girl.'

'I agree totally.' Hugh ran a hand down his face and released a long sigh. 'But can you imagine the pain of arguing in court about whether Ivy was lost

or hiding—or—or whether she's beautiful or deformed?'

'No,' Jo admitted, shuddering. Hugh was right. It
would be horrendous. 'And I guess I'll just have to
live with all that rubbish about Bindi Creek and the
claim that I wouldn't know how to care for anything
except wombats. But it—it's—'

She clamped her mouth shut to stop herself from
swearing. If she wasn't careful she would be in tears
again.

'I doubt anyone will believe that about you, Jo.'

'But then there's the problem of the engagement
announcement,' she said. 'I assume you set Priscilla
straight last night, but what about everyone else?
What are you going to tell them?'

'About our plans to marry?'

The question seemed to resonate in the room as if
a gong had been struck. Hugh continued to lean
against the table, not moving at all.

But a tiny smile sparked in his eyes.

And a sudden shiver rippled down Jo's spine.

'I don't know,' he said at last, letting the words
roll out slowly. 'Maybe we shouldn't get too uptight
about denying our wedding plans. After all, it's New
Year's Eve.'

Jo gulped to try to rid herself of the sensation that
she'd swallowed a marble. 'What's New Year's Eve
got to do with it?'

His eyes shimmered with an intensely intimate glow.

And for some inexplicable reason Jo couldn't breathe.

This was ridiculous. Anyone would think she and Hugh had something going—an *understanding*—that they were actually contemplating marriage.

And, just to make things worse, her skin flashed hot and cold as she remembered the way he'd kissed her, the way she'd kissed him back.

His mouth tilted into his familiar heartbreaking smile. 'Today marks an important milestone. We've known each other for an entire week, Jo.'

A week. Had it only been such a short time? She felt as if she'd known Hugh for ever.

He was still smiling. 'So it wouldn't be rushing things if we made our engagement official, would it?'

Of course he was teasing her. He had to be. *The cad.* She wasn't in the mood for playing games.

It wasn't very sporting of him. Even if he was the future Earl of Rychester and the best-looking man in Greater London, and even if his ancestors had been bedding their serving wenches for centuries, Lord Hugh Strickland should know better than to play around with his daughter's twenty-first century nanny.

Her emotions were already fragile this morning and now she could feel her anger shooting high— volcano style. It would serve Hugh right if she called his bluff.

Come to think of it, why shouldn't she? It would

do him the world of good if he got some of his own back.

With a coolness that reflected nothing of the havoc inside her, she threw back her shoulders and looked straight into his cheeky smiling eyes. 'What a terrific idea, Hugh. We can make a formal engagement announcement at your friend Rupert's party tonight. Actually, why stop there? I'll alert the Country Women's Association in Bindi Creek to be ready to cater for our wedding reception. That would be fine with you, wouldn't it?'

She allowed herself a small, self-satisfied smirk as she waited for his reaction.

But, when it came, it wasn't quite what she expected.

Hugh didn't laugh. He didn't chuckle. He didn't even grin.

He suddenly looked impossibly serious. Colour stained his high cheekbones and he stared at her with a breath-robbing intensity.

For lo-o-ong seconds they stood watching each other, while Jo's heart pounded and her preposterous counter to his joke echoed back at her from every corner of the room.

What was the matter with Hugh? He must know she wasn't serious. He knew she was going home at the end of next week.

Suddenly overcome by the tension that seemed to have seized them both, she dropped her gaze and stared at her hands instead. For heaven's sake, someone had to break the silence. She took a deep breath. 'And if tonight's going to be the big night, you've only got the rest of the day to come up with a spectacular proposal.' And then she chanced an anxious glance his way.

And at last he reacted.

For one brief moment he frowned. Then his right eyebrow arched as he flicked back the ribbed cuff of his black cashmere sweater and looked at his wristwatch. 'So we have till midnight?' Without warning, he sent her a roguish smile. 'That means we still have fourteen and a half hours. Plenty of time for me to propose.'

Jo gulped. Was she seriously overreacting, or was this nonsense getting completely out of hand? But as she struggled to think of a response, the front door bell rang.

And Hugh's merriment vanished. 'Humphries will get that,' he said, suddenly businesslike. 'If either of us answers the front door we might find our photo in the paper tomorrow.'

'Really?' It hadn't occurred to Jo that there might be paparazzi lurking outside Hugh's house. She was standing near a window where the curtains had been drawn open, and she couldn't resist taking a quick peek.

'Jo, stay away.'

Too late! There was a bright flash from the foot path.

She jumped back. 'I'm sorry, Hugh. I didn't think they would notice me up here.'

From the hall came the sound of the front door slamming, and then a man's voice. 'Damned press. Every last one of them should be hanged, drawn and quartered.'

'But not by you, Felix,' a woman's voice said. 'There was no need to swing at that young man with your umbrella.'

'Ah,' said Hugh with a strange look that expressed a mixture of pain and virtuous duty, as if he'd swallowed unpalatable medicine that he'd been told was good for him. 'Now you'll have the pleasure of meeting my parents.'

'Already? I thought they were coming up from Devon?'

Hugh managed a tight smile. 'By helicopter.'

*Oh, good grief.* Jo pressed damp palms against her thighs and found herself standing to attention. She didn't feel ready to meet the earl and his wife. Not before breakfast.

To add to her surprise, Hugh crossed to her side and slipped a friendly arm around her shoulders. 'Don't look so worried, Jo. They'll love you. You're the daughter-in-law they've always wanted.'

'Stop it, Hugh. How can you keep joking about that?' She was furious that he could be so playful about such a serious subject. How insensitive of him to tease her now, when he must know she was stressed to the max!

Even if Hugh's parents hadn't read the column in the paper they were sure to have heard about it. They would know by now that she was the incompetent, careless nanny who'd managed to lose their grand-child between bouts of leaping into bed with their son.

If only she could scurry downstairs to join Ivy and Regina in the kitchen.

'Oh, God, Hugh,' she whispered in sudden panic. 'How do I address your parents?'

'Call them Felix and Rowena,' he whispered back.

'Hugh!'

He grinned. 'Or Lord and Lady Rychester—whichever takes your fancy.'

She half-expected Humphries to come to the door and announce the earl and his wife, the way butlers did in movies, but when the door opened a somewhat matronly woman hurried into the dining room and Jo had no chance of getting her knocking knees under control.

'Hugh, darling.'

'Mother.'

Holding out her arms, the woman gave Hugh a kiss and an enthusiastic motherly hug.

Jo bit back an involuntary gasp of surprise. She wasn't sure what she'd expected Lady Rychester to look like—probably someone with a regal air and a haughty, cold beauty like Priscilla's. She certainly hadn't anticipated a woman who was shorter than herself, almost plump, with soft salt and pepper curls and warm, smiling brown eyes.

Hugh's mother even had an outdoorsy glow about her. She was not unlike how Jo's own mother might look if Margie Berry ever had the funds to dress in classic black trousers, a cream silk blouse teamed with a Hermes scarf, and pearl studs in her ears and a single strand of perfectly matched pearls at her throat.

Jo had barely got over that shock before Hugh's father, who'd been having a word with Humphries, strode into the room.

The earl was a different story—a taller, thinner, more stiff-upper-lipped version of Hugh. His eyes were very dark, almost piercing jade-black, and they made him look more than a little frightening.

Lord Rychester greeted Hugh with a grunt and a handshake. 'Had to fight through a pack of vultures to get to your front door,' he grumbled.

And then he fixed his sharp-eyed attention squarely on Jo.

# CHAPTER EIGHT

HUGH intervened quickly. 'Mother, Father, I'd like you to meet Joanna Berry. As you know, she's kindly come with me from Australia to help Ivy settle in. I couldn't have managed without her.'

Hugh's mother clasped Jo's hand between hers. 'I'm delighted to meet you, Joanna. It's so kind of you to help Hugh.'

'How do you do, Lady Rychester?' Jo said and she wondered if a curtsey was in order.

'Pleased to meet you, Joanna,' the earl said more formally.

Jo offered her hand. 'How do you do, Lord Rychester?'

Oh, heavens, this felt seriously scary.

How had a chance meeting with Hugh in her family's humble shop in Bindi Creek lead her to this?

'My dear, I can't imagine what you must think of our outrageous British press,' said Hugh's mother. 'I'm so sorry.'

Jo could have kissed her. 'Thank you. It's very kind of you to say so.'

'We've had a dreadful morning,' admitted Hugh.

'Damn tabloids,' muttered the earl and his piercing gaze speared Jo. 'Don't give them a victory, lass.

You're not going to charge off home to Australia because of this, are you?'

'Not yet, sir.'

'Jo hasn't even managed so much as a cup of tea this morning,' said Hugh.

'Can't have that,' said his father. 'Let's get a fresh pot. I could do with a cup.'

Hugh smiled. 'I'll organise fresh provisions.'

Lady Rychester was casting a curious glance towards the door leading upstairs. 'I'm dying to meet Ivy,' she said. 'Is she awake?'

'She's in the kitchen,' Hugh told her, 'eating a soft boiled egg with toast soldiers.'

His mother's eyes shone. 'Oh, the little darling.' She turned to Jo. 'Is she very shy?'

'No, not really.' The eager light in the other woman's eyes touched Jo's heart. She'd been so caught up with feeling nervous that she'd temporarily forgotten how important this meeting must be for Ivy's grandmother. Now she felt a rush of empathy for her.

'I'll fetch Ivy, shall I?' asked Hugh with a proud smile that advertised how very much he was enjoying his new role as a father.

'Darling, please do.'

It was only after Hugh had left that Jo remembered Ivy was still in her pyjamas. Worse, her hair wasn't brushed and her face was probably covered in egg.

*Cringe.* Hugh's parents might be prepared to overlook the preposterous claims in the newspaper, but they would be less charitable when they saw evidence of the nanny's incompetence with their own eyes.

Nervously, she asked them if they would like to sit down. But they had only just taken their seats when a piping voice could be heard coming up the stairs.

'Have I really got an English grandmother, Daddy?'

'Yes, don't you remember? Jo and I told you about her yesterday. She's upstairs.'

'Is she a fairy grandmother?'

'No, just a regular grandmother.'

'A hairy grandmother?' Ivy was giggling at her own joke.

Jo held her breath. When Ivy got overexcited she could be quite silly.

'A scary grandmother?' Ivy giggled again as she and Hugh walked into the room, hand in hand.

Despite the pyjamas and the tumbled curls, Jo thought the little girl looked very appealing. Her face was scrubbed clean. *Thank you, Regina.* Her lively eyes were dancing with merriment and no amount of stray curls could mar her exquisite features.

But when Ivy saw Hugh's parents she came to a halt and Jo was reminded of the morning when she and Hugh had arrived at Agate Downs and the child had been overawed to see strangers.

'Ivy,' she said, holding out an encouraging hand.

'Your grandmother and grandfather have come all the way to London especially to meet you.'

But Ivy seemed to have frozen to the spot. She clung to Hugh's hand and eyed her grandparents from a safe distance, assessing them with solemn, frowning wariness.

Hugh looked a little out of his depth. 'Come on, Ivy, say hello.'

'Hello,' she said and then she lowered her gaze and dropped her bottom lip.

Sensing an awkward moment that could escalate into an uncomfortable scene, Jo jumped to her feet. 'I have a good idea. Why don't we take Grandmother upstairs to show her your new bedroom? You can introduce her to Howard and Baby and you can show her some of your nice new clothes.' *And I can tidy you up and get you dressed.*

Ivy seemed to think this over.

The little minx, thought Jo. She's playing with us.

But suddenly the little girl took a delighted skip forward. 'Yes,' she said, eyes twinkling once more. 'That's a very good idea.' She held out an imperious hand to a rather bemused Lady Rychester. 'Come on, Grandmother. Come with Jo and me and we'll show you my lovely new bedroom.'

'Well done, Jo. I couldn't have managed without you. I categorically *could not* have survived this day without your help.'

It was mid-afternoon and Hugh was sprawled on

a sitting room sofa, where he'd collapsed the minute his parents had left to visit friends in Mayfair.

Jo, curled in an armchair opposite him, was rather stunned by the enormous relief Hugh had expressed.

'I can't believe they took Ivy with them,' he said.

'They want to show off their granddaughter,' she responded. 'They're absolutely smitten with her. It's wonderful, isn't it?'

'The amazing thing is the adoration seems to be mutual. Ivy really took to them, didn't she?'

'That's not so surprising, Hugh. I thought your parents were rather sweet. I was afraid of your father at first, but he's a softie underneath that upper class crust.'

'He's a softie around you,' Hugh amended. 'You have no idea how differently my father behaved today compared to the way he usually treats my women.'

'Perhaps that's because I am *not* one of your girl-friends.' Jo hurled a cushion at him.

Hugh caught it and hugged it to his chest and then he grinned at her. 'You might not be mine yet.' He glanced at the clock on the mantelpiece. 'But it's half past three. Only nine hours left till midnight. Time's running out, Jo.'

She let out a wail of impatience. 'I'm getting tired of this ridiculous game.'

'Then perhaps I should propose to you now.'

*Yeah, right.*

'For heaven's sake, Hugh, give that subject a

miss!' She hurled another cushion his way but, to her horror, it went sailing over his head and knocked a beautiful porcelain vase from the sofa table behind him.

She leapt to her feet, appalled by the mess she'd made. The vase had broken into three pieces and rose petals, flower heads and stems were scattered in a sodden heap. And, of course, there was a pool of water soaking into the white wool carpet.

'I'm so sorry. I'll get something to mop up the mess. Was that vase expensive? It's not Ming or anything is it?'

Hugh jumped from the sofa and caught her hand as she hurried past. 'It's Meissen, but don't worry.' Holding her hand tightly, he drew her close. Within a heartbeat her face was only inches from his.

'Hugh, I—I've got to get a bucket or—'

'Or nothing.'

Jo gulped for air. Up this close, Hugh was breathtaking. Literally. 'But the carpet. That stain should be treated quickly.'

'There's another matter that requires more urgent attention.'

'What—what's that?'

His hand slid down, pressing into her lower back, bringing her pelvis suddenly against his. 'I desperately need you, Jo.'

*Oh, God.* His words plunged straight between her legs and she felt a shocking, violent eruption of desire.

With one hand holding her close, Hugh used the other to trace a line with his fingertip along her jaw, down her throat to the V neckline of her sweater, and his green eyes burned with such wicked, devilish heat she felt her breasts swell and her nipples grow tight with unbearable longing.

So quickly. Just like that. She'd become an incendiary bomb about to explode. If Hugh kissed her, if he lifted her sweater, if he touched her anywhere *intimate* she would disintegrate. She'd be lost.

'No,' she managed to whisper. 'Don't.'

'Come upstairs,' he urged and his voice was low— a hot chocolate, super-seductive rumble. 'You want me, Jo. Don't you?'

Of course she did, but that wasn't the point. 'Please, no. Let me go.' Shoving her hands into his chest, she pushed him away from her.

And to her relief as well as her dismay, he did exactly what she asked. He let her go.

Breathless, panting, she staggered backwards, almost overbalancing.

Hugh looked as if he might follow her and she held up a shaking hand. 'Hold it.'

His eyes narrowed.

'I think you're getting a little confused, Lord Strickland. I'm here to look after your daughter, not to be your girlfriend.'

'Jo, don't be angry. Just be honest with yourself. And with me.'

'I'm sorry, Hugh, but why shouldn't I be angry?

Sex was not part of our agreement. Maybe you're used to having the pick of whichever English girl you fancy, but despite what's reported in newspapers here, Aussies aren't all that impressed by titles.'

He stood very still with his shoulders squared. His chest expanded and compressed, as if he was breathing hard. His eyes smouldered with dark, banked heat. 'What if I were to tell you that I think I love you?'

*Oh, no, don't do that to me.* Jo gaped at him, too stunned to come up with an answer.

In his eyes she saw naked emotion that made her want to cry.

How had this happened? Something was wrong. She was the vulnerable one. She didn't have the power to hurt Hugh Strickland. But he could break her heart.

On the verge of tears, she pressed her lips tightly together as she tried to get her emotions in check. 'Why? Why do you have to be who you are?'

'What the hell does that mean?'

She released a desperate strangled sigh. 'If you were an everyday average Englishman, it would be different.'

'You mean you might be upstairs naked and in bed with me right now?'

Jo gulped. 'Yes…perhaps.'

His frown was accompanied by a troubled smile. He scratched the back of his neck. 'Excuse me, Miss Berry, but aren't you contradicting yourself?'

It was Jo's turn to frown. 'No, I don't think so.'

'But one minute you're telling me you're not impressed by titles and the next you're saying that my title is so damned impressive it's scaring you off.'

Finding herself suddenly at sea, she flapped her hands helplessly. 'There's no point in discussing this. I'm going upstairs. To *my* room. I—I need to paint my nails for tonight.'

'By all means.' A weary smile flitted across Hugh's face. 'You'll want to look your very best for tonight.'

Confusion stormed inside her as she hurried upstairs. What was the matter with her? In her secret heart she'd been hoping for a romance with Hugh, and now that she had the chance she was running scared like a terrified child.

Running scared because Hugh thought he might love her—which was exactly what she'd hoped, but had never dreamed was possible.

It wasn't possible. Hugh was confusing lust with love. Very soon he would come to his senses and realise his mistake and she would be grateful for her lucky escape.

In her room, she took out the small bottle of dark berry-red nail polish to match the beautiful dress Hugh had bought her. One thing Hugh had said was right. Tonight she needed to look as glamorous as possible if she was to have any hope of measuring up to his friends. But her hands were still shaking so badly she had no chance of applying the polish.

Ivy and Hugh's parents would be home soon and then she would be busy getting Ivy ready for the party and she'd have no time for herself.

Acting on a sudden desperate whim, she snatched up the bottle and tore back downstairs, not glancing to the sitting room where she'd left Hugh but continuing all the way to the kitchen, where Regina was ironing and listening to the radio.

'I'm sorry to bother you, Regina.' Jo held up the little red pot of polish. 'I was wondering if you could lend me a steady hand.'

'Heavens, love, it's a while since I painted a fingernail, but I'll give it a try. It makes a change from ironing.'

After switching off the iron and lowering the volume on the radio, Regina pulled out a chair at the kitchen table. 'Let's see if I still have the knack.'

'It's so good of you. I'm too nervous and shaky,' Jo admitted.

'Don't be nervous about going to Rupert's house,' Regina said as she shook the bottle. 'He's the loveliest, kindest man.' Regina sent Jo a sudden shrewd glance. 'That Priscilla Mostly-Tart won't be there, will she?'

'Priscilla *who?*'

'Mosley-Hart. Sorry, Jo. I know I have a hide to call her names.'

But Jo couldn't resist a small smile. 'I don't think she'll be there. She's out of favour. If she turns up,

Hugh will have her clapped in irons and taken to the Tower.'

'About time Hugh came to his senses.' Regina painted a steady stripe of crimson on to Jo's thumbnail. 'You have lovely hands.'

'Thank you.'

As she finished the first nail, the housekeeper let out a laughing shout of triumph. 'Look at that. Perfect. I haven't lost my knack.' She dipped the little brush back into the polish. 'Just relax and enjoy yourself tonight, ducks. I have a very good feeling in my bones. I think you'll come home on cloud nine and won't that be a wonderful way to start the New Year?'

## CHAPTER NINE

HUGH had never felt more uptight than he did that evening as Humphries drove him with Jo and Ivy to the Eliots' house. His feelings for Jo had thrown him into a complete tailspin. He'd never been so undone.

He'd fallen in love—*really* in love—and it was no fun at all. He couldn't imagine a condition that rendered a man more helpless. More joyous. More tormented.

He was racked by gut-wrenching pre-party nerves and he hadn't felt this tense about taking a girl to a party since his teenage years.

During the past week there'd been times when he'd convinced himself that his feelings were returned. He'd caught Jo looking at him with a special soft light in her eyes. He'd seen the way his sudden appearance in a room could make flushes of colour come and go in her cheeks. And when he'd kissed her, her lips and limbs had responded with a trembling, sweet desperation that couldn't be faked.

She was such a contrast to Priscilla who'd been so in love with his title and money that she'd been willing to gamble everything in a bid to win him as a husband.

What bitter-sweet irony it was that Jo had thrown

149

his riches and privileges at him as her reasons for keeping him at bay.

'Oh, look.' Jo was craning her neck to look out through the car window. 'I think I can see snow.' She turned back to him, her eyes shining. 'Is it, Hugh? Is it snow?'

He blinked and saw fluffy white flakes spinning and gleaming in the glare of street lights and head-lights. 'That's snow all right. Haven't you ever seen it?'

'No,' Jo and Ivy answered together and they gave little squeals of delight as they leaned forward, watching with mouths and eyes wide open.

'It's just beautiful,' said Jo.

But her happiness depressed Hugh. He glared at the pretty flakes. In his current mood the snow seemed to emphasise the vast differences between Jo's world and his.

'I'm afraid most of the snow we get in London usually melts or turns to slush almost as soon as it reaches the road,' he felt compelled to warn her.

But she wasn't going to be put off.

'It doesn't matter.' Her face was flushed with the enchantment of it all. 'Look Ivy, it's real snow. Now I'll be able to tell everyone at home that I've seen it.'

Hugh swallowed a sigh.

When they arrived at the Eliots' the white flakes were still drifting softly about them and as they stepped out of the car the scene before them was picture perfect—the Eliots' lovely house with lights glowing from every window, the falling snow outside and the promise of warmth and gaiety within.

And then the door opened and a blast of music from a dance band greeted them and Rupert, who'd beaten his butler to the door, was grinning broadly and urging them to hurry in out of the cold.

Inside, they were immediately surrounded by a grand and welcoming spectacle—warmly tapestried walls, dazzling chandeliers, glittering mirrors and pieces of silver, beautiful flower arrangements and polished parquet floors designed especially for dancing feet.

Introductions were made amidst a great deal of laughter and happy chatter accompanied by hugs and kisses. The Eliots' butler hurried to help Ivy and Jo with their coats. Jo smiled as she thanked him and then she turned slowly, looking a little overwhelmed as she took in her surroundings. And Hugh felt as if he'd turned to stone.

He stood stock still, rooted to the spot by the sight of Jo in her lovely red dress.

She was beyond beautiful.

The deep crimson gown was perfect for her. Its colour offset her dark brown hair and eyes and highlighted the rosy tints in her complexion and the delicious deep red of her mouth. The dress's fabric was soft, skimming close to her figure without clinging. The cut was daring, with a deep plunging back and a tantalising low neckline, which somehow, mercifully, kept Jo's modesty intact.

The combination of boldness and decorum sent fire shooting to his loins.

'Is something the matter, Hugh?' High colour sprang into her cheeks. 'Don't you like the dress?'

He tried to answer, but his heart seemed to fill his throat.

'What about my dress, Daddy?' demanded Ivy, not to be outdone. 'Do you like it?'

He dragged his gaze from Jo to his daughter in her new winter dress of emerald-green velvet that matched her sparkling green eyes. 'It's beautiful, poppet. You both look—' He had to take a breath. 'You both look like princesses.' He turned to his best friend. 'Don't they, Rupert?'

'Absolutely gorgeous.' Rupert shot a knowing look Hugh's way. 'So gorgeous I'm going to have to ask you both for a dance.'

Ivy was suddenly shy and turned to whisper to Jo, who gave her a reassuring pat.

'Ivy's worried because she doesn't know how to dance,' she told Rupert.

'Then I shall teach you,' he said to Ivy with a charming grin as he held out his hand to her. 'Come on, let's go.'

Which left Hugh and Jo alone.

A waiter offered them a tray of drinks and they made their selections—champagne for Jo and Scotch for Hugh—and for a short while they stood together without talking, while they watched Rupert take Ivy's hand and spin her around. Within seconds the child was beaming with delight.

'Oh, there you are,' called a voice. It was Anne Eliot, so there were more introductions and happy chatter. 'I thought we'd let the children party with us for an hour or so and then our nanny will take them upstairs,' Anne explained. 'Don't worry about Ivy. There are plenty of children here to keep her happy and plenty of beds for when she gets tired.'

She dragged them off then, so that Jo could be introduced to other guests and, as Hugh might have expected of guests at the Eliots', no one raised the question of the newspaper column and it was all very pleasant—until Jack Soames asked Jo to dance.

She responded after only the slightest hesitation and as she and Jack headed out on to the dance floor Hugh toyed with the idea of asking one of the other women to be his dancing partner, but he was hopelessly mesmerised by Jo. Leaning against a marble pillar, he clutched his glass of whisky and watched her dancing and smiling—and suffered.

Once or twice, Jo sent a brief, anxious look his way, but on the whole she paid a great deal of attention to Jack and she looked as if she was enjoying herself. Very much. Almost as much as her partner.

'That Jo of yours is charming.'

Hugh started as Rupert's voice sounded close beside him.

Rupert raised a sandy eyebrow. 'You're not yourself tonight, old chap.'

Hugh grunted and muttered a deliberately incomprehensible reply.

'You're not letting that idiot from *Nelson's Column* bother you, are you?'

'No, not at all, but it's been hard for Jo. I blame bloody Priscilla for the whole thing.'

'I hear old Mosley-Hart's lost all his money,' Rupert said. 'Some crazy get rich quick investment that went belly up.'

So that explained why Priscilla had been so dead keen to get herself engaged when he'd returned from Australia, thought Hugh. It was all about money.

'I must say your little Ivy is absolutely delightful,' Rupert added in an obvious attempt to soothe his friend.

This time Hugh smiled. 'She's fantastic, isn't she? I'm so lucky. I still can't quite believe I'm a father, though. But we've gotten to know each other very quickly. I adore her.'

His friend didn't reply at first. 'I take it you're referring to your daughter?'

'Naturally.' Hugh felt his face flush and shot Rupert a warning look.

'But if I'd been talking about Joanna Berry, your answer would have been the same, wouldn't it?' Rupert said with clear disregard for Hugh's warning.

Hugh opened his mouth to deny it. But what was

the point? Rupert was his oldest friend and could read him like a book. 'Yes,' he said softly and then he downed his Scotch in a swift gulp.

Rupert signalled for a waiter to bring them fresh drinks and, once they'd made their selections, he said, 'Unless I've lost my ability to sum up a person at a first meeting, I'd say you've hit the jackpot this time, old fellow.'

Hugh frowned.

'Don't pretend you don't know who I'm talking about.'

'So you like Jo?' Hugh couldn't resist asking; the question mattered a great deal.

'Yes, and I don't just mean that I like the look of her.' Rupert took a sip of wine. 'Although it's hard to ignore that lovely figure.'

Hugh glared at him. 'When will you ever give up? You've been a stirrer since our school days.'

Rupert smiled. 'Actually, she's very different from the women you usually mistreat. No offence, Hugh, but I consider that a plus.'

Hugh knew what Rupert meant. They were both familiar with his tendency to be blind-sided by women of rare physical beauty and his habit of moving on as soon as he got to know them.

But then he'd met Jo and he hadn't been swept away by stunning looks. He'd been pleasantly charmed by a pretty girl with a sweet, warm smile. And now, after a week in her company, he was completely spellbound by her rare and beautiful spirit.

For him, Jo's ordinary prettiness had blossomed and deepened into a more stirring, more compelling beauty than any he'd encountered.

'I'll tell you something else I like about your nanny,' said Rupert.

'Mention her body again and you put our lifetime friendship in jeopardy.'

Rupert chuckled. 'Seriously, I like what she's done to you.'

'Done to me? I'm a wreck.'

'Exactly. And I'm very pleased to see it. It's about time.' From behind rimless spectacles Rupert's clever blue eyes shone with a beguiling mixture of sympathy and delight. 'You've never felt this miserable over a girl before, have you?'

'No.' After a bit, Hugh said, 'I love her.'

'Does she know how you feel?'

'Yes. No. Sort of.' He stared at the drink in his hand. 'I've made a complete hash of trying to tell her.'

'Well, there's no need to rush these things.'

'There is, actually. She's going back to Australia at the end of next week.'

Rupert lifted both eyebrows. 'I'll admit a deadline injects a certain degree of urgency.'

'Yes. I've got to pull a rabbit out of a hat.'

Hugh sighed. Rupert and Anne had it all—a relationship that was as secure and constant as it was passionate. And deep down he was certain that he could have that with Jo. If only he could find the right words…

Rupert's hand clasped his shoulder. 'Be careful, my friend. A proposal of marriage isn't the same as securing one of your business deals. Women don't respond well to pressure.'

Hugh wasn't so sure about that as he watched the couples out on the dance floor. Hal Ramsay was cutting in to replace Jo's partner and, as soon as she began to dance with Hal, the music slowed to something soft and bluesy.

Next minute Hal was drawing her in—and his hand, damn it, was dangerously close to her lovely bare back. For crying out loud, the man had a wife of his own and Jo was smiling at him as if he'd offered her the sun and the stars.

What a pity Hugh was spoiling everything.

Jo didn't know what to make of his behaviour tonight. Why wasn't he dancing and having fun? She'd been sure that the dashing and charming Lord Strickland would be the life of the party.

She was having a great time. It was so exciting to be in such a lovely house, wearing such a beautiful, beautiful gown. She felt totally welcome. The Eliots were charming and friendly and so were their guests. No one so far had been snobbish or condescending. No one had mentioned *Nelson's Column*. No one had asked awkward questions about her relationship with Hugh.

But, instead of enjoying himself, Hugh was standing aloof, watching her with the frowning stare of an old maidish chaperon.

Well, maybe not old maidish. Not Hugh. He looked far too manly and gorgeous in his superb black tails. Brooding and moody might be a better description.

What was the matter with him? Surely he wasn't upset with her? She couldn't believe that his teasing about proposals and engagements was serious. As for his comment about loving her—she would be naïve and foolish to think that had been any more than smooth words rolling off the tongue of a skilful seducer. They were worlds apart and she had to remember that.

She was determined to have fun this evening in spite of Hugh's sulky mood. Tonight was a one-off chance for an Aussie chick in London to check out the way the upper-crust partied. She owed it to the girls back in the office to soak up every glamorous detail so she could give them a blow by blow report when she—

'Excuse me.'

Hugh's voice stopped her thoughts and her dancing mid-track.

Her head jerked up and her eyes met his. Green. Gorgeous. Black-fringed. Oh, man. Her heart began a strange little dance, completely out of time with the music.

Hugh tapped her partner's shoulder. 'I'm sorry,

Hal, but your time's up,' he said, flashing a tight-lipped version of his charming smile. 'My turn.'

Hot and cold shivers darted over Jo's skin and she felt an urgent need to protest, or to find an excuse to avoid close contact with Hugh. The dance was about to end, wasn't it? Shouldn't she check on Ivy?

But her partner was politely stepping away and within a heartbeat Hugh had usurped his place, taking her hand in his and placing his other at her waist and then drawing her close.

Too close. She couldn't breathe.

The dance was no more than a simple slow shuffle in time to the music. Nevertheless she stumbled.

'I'm sorry,' said Hugh. 'Did I trip you?'

She shook her head, suddenly too breathless, too anxious to speak. Oh, dear heaven, why did she have to react to Hugh this way? Why couldn't she be calm and sensible, the way she'd been when she'd danced with the other men? She was quite an uninhibited dancer normally. Now, for the life of her, she couldn't untangle her feet.

She bumped into Hugh again and the impact of their bodies was only slight, but that was all it took— a brief brush of his chest and thigh—to set off flash-points of reaction all over her.

Hugh leaned back a little and studied her face. 'You look a little pale, Jo. Perhaps you need a drink?'

'Thank you.' It would be a blessed relief to stop dancing.

His hand settled at her waist as he steered her from the dance floor and she could feel the burning imprint of his thumb on the bare skin at her lower back.

'Why don't you try a brandy?' He looked about for a waiter. 'It's supposed to have medicinal benefits.'

But now that he wasn't touching her Jo felt more composed. 'I don't need brandy, thank you. I'd just like some water, please.'

He came back from the bar with a tall crystal tumbler filled with ice and water and, as he watched her drink it, a worried frown creased his forehead.

'That's better,' she said, forcing a smile as she finished half of it. 'This is a lovely party, Hugh.'

He nodded. 'Anne and Rupert always put on a good show for New Year's Eve.'

Jo looked towards the foot of the staircase where a young fresh-faced woman had gathered several of the children. 'I think that might be the Eliots' nanny getting the children ready to go upstairs now. I'll go and find Ivy and make sure she understands what's happening.'

'Good idea. I'll come with you.'

That wasn't quite what she'd had in mind.

Ivy and another little girl were playing peek-a-boo around a pillar at the side of the dance floor.

'But I'm not ready to go to sleep yet,' she protested when she saw Hugh and Jo approaching.

'All the other children are going upstairs now,' Hugh told her.

'No, I don't want to!' Ivy's bottom lip projected in a familiar pout.

Time for some gentle coercion, Jo decided. 'Wouldn't you like to sleep upstairs with your new little friends?'

'In the same room?' Ivy asked, suddenly interested. 'Like Tilly and Grace?'

'Yes,' said Jo, although she was quite sure that the Eliots' nursery would be nothing like the humble bedroom her little sisters shared.

Remarkably, that was all it took for Ivy to agree.

'After everything else that's happened this week I'm surprised Ivy remembers Tilly and Grace,' Jo said as they watched the chattering children climb the stairs.

Hugh smiled. 'You'll have to admit that your family's rather memorable.'

Something in the way he said that lifted fine hairs on Jo's skin. She looked up at him and he smiled again, but it wasn't a particularly convincing smile. She was sure she could sense a shadow of sadness behind it.

She was afraid to ask, but then the words spilled out anyhow. 'Is something the matter, Hugh?'

His eyes pierced her. 'I need to talk to you, Jo.'

'OK.' She felt suddenly breathless. 'I'm listening.'

'Not here.'

Her heart hammered as she looked about her. The Eliots' nanny and her little flock of children were almost at the top of the stairs. To her right, Anne

Eliot was helping an elderly white-haired woman into a chair and offering her a glass of sherry. A couple nearby were sharing an apparently uproariously funny joke. No one was paying any attention to Hugh or Jo. 'You can talk here, can't you?'

'No,' he said, reaching for her hand. 'Come upstairs with me.'

'Upstairs?' she squeaked.

'There's a little conservatory on the next floor, and there's something I want to show you.'

Rolling her eyes at him, she made a nervous attempt at a joke. 'That's not very original, Lord Strickland. What have you got up there? Etchings?'

His mouth quirked as he gave her hand a tug. 'I promise this is all above board. It will only take five minutes.'

'Oh, very well.'

At the first landing, he pushed open a door to the right and they entered a small informal dining room. Hugh didn't turn the light on, but on the far side of the room pale moonlight spilled through a snow-covered glass-roofed conservatory on to potted palms and flowers.

'Wow!' Jo forgot to be nervous as she walked towards the glass-walled room. 'This is so pretty.' She stepped into the conservatory and was met by the scent of roses. She looked up and saw enchanting little banks of snow lying against the ribs that joined the glass panels—and, higher, the moon shining through a break in the clouds.

But then she turned back to Hugh and in the moon-washed shadows she saw the look of deep intent in his eyes. Her heart leapt. 'Oh, God, Hugh, why have you brought me here? You're not going to try to seduce me again?'

He held up his hands. 'I'm on my very best behaviour, Jo. I want to ask you to marry me.'

She felt a slam of panic. 'But you can't. You mustn't keep this silly joke going.'

'I love you.'

'Don't say that.'

'Why shouldn't I love you?' Hugh stepped towards her and his voice was husky with emotion. 'You're a miracle, Jo Berry.'

She mustn't let herself listen to such temptation. 'I'm going home in a week, I'm only here to help you with Ivy.'

He took her by the shoulders. 'This has nothing to do with my daughter. I want you for myself.'

She wanted to cry. Her dream had come true. But now that it had, it felt terribly wrong. She felt a rush of tears. This was so surreal.

'Why can't you believe me?' Hugh whispered.

Wriggling her shoulders out of his grasp, she took two steps back. 'It—it's too much like a fantasy—a fairy tale. I'm Jo Berry from Bindi Creek and you're—you're Prince Charming. I shouldn't even be here at this party, dressed in this gorgeous gown and dancing with your blue blood friends. I—I should be with the Eliots' nanny, taking the children to the toilet or settling them down to sleep.'

Hugh ploughed a frantic hand through his hair. 'You're letting that damned *Nelson's Column* get to you. Either that or you're deliberately underselling yourself.'

'I'm being realistic.'

'How's this for realism?'

Hugh took something from his breast pocket. It was difficult at first to see what he held in his hand, but then he moved slightly and she caught the unmistakable sparkle of gemstones.

Her heart jumped as if a shot had been fired.

'This was my grandmother's engagement ring,' he said. 'I've never offered it to another woman, but I very much want you to have it, Jo.'

This couldn't be happening. She was dreaming. She had to be.

'There are five stones,' Hugh continued in his low, deeply beautiful voice. 'Three diamonds and two rubies and, according to the story my grandmother liked to tell, the five stones represent five words. *Will you be my wife?*'

The conservatory seemed to swim before her.

'Jo,' Hugh whispered, 'please say something.'

She blurted the first words that came into her head. 'I think you've taken this too far.'

'What?' The little jewellery box in his hand shook. 'You can't really believe this is still a joke.'

She pressed a hand against her clamouring heart.

'What else can it be? Think about it, Hugh. You've already hinted at our engagement once when you didn't mean it. That's pretty fast work for a couple who've only known each other a week. Maybe it's getting to be a bad habit—a quick fix solution. How can I be confident that you really mean it this time?'

He gave an impatient shake of his head.

'A marriage proposal! That's for life, Hugh. It would make more sense if you propositioned me again. Can't you see that?'

Surely she'd made perfect sense. Why was he being so stubborn? 'Can't you see how rushed this is?' She felt compelled to fling him her trump card. 'After all, you still have Priscilla's things in your bedroom.'

He frowned. 'When were you in my room?'

'This afternoon.'

She'd gone there after Regina had painted her nails. She'd felt a sudden need to apologise to Hugh for the immature way she'd rebuffed him. And she'd decided to tell him the truth...that she fancied the pants off him. She could be persuaded to change her mind...

But when she couldn't find him in the lounge she'd gone upstairs and she'd stepped into his bedroom...

'You still have a box of Priscilla's things on the floor just inside your bedroom door,' she told him now. 'Her name is marked very clearly on the side.'

Hugh groaned softly. 'Humphries was going to deliver that box to her but with all the phone calls and nonsense in the press he's been distracted. I'm sorry.'

'I'm not sorry. It was a timely wake up call for me.'

He gave another impatient shake of his head. 'I was never in love with Priscilla, Jo. Even before I learned about Ivy, I had realised that Priscilla and I were headed for misery. And that was before she walked out on me at the very time I needed her support.'

'Well, I can't help wondering if you'd change your mind about me too,' said Jo. 'What guarantee do I have that in a month or two there won't be a box of my things waiting for Humphries to deliver to me?'

She swallowed and bothersome tears sprang to her eyes. 'I'm sorry, Hugh. I'm not prepared to take a gamble on that.'

In the moonlight she saw the way his face stiffened. 'Is that your final word?' he asked.

Every part of her wanted to say no.

He remained standing very still. Very British and stiff—and he looked more dashing and gorgeous than ever in his dark formal evening clothes.

'Is it your final word?' he asked again.

She opened her mouth to say yes, and then she shut it. She thought of her mum and the wistful dream that had sent her flying here to London with Hugh. And then she thought of the box of frilly negligées in Hugh's room and she imagined the words Joanna Berry written in black felt pen on the side.

'Yes,' she said. 'It's my final word.'

Hugh looked down at the ring in his hand and then quickly closed his fist over it. 'Forgive me for taking up your time.' With a grim, tight face he slipped the ring into his pocket.

He made a movement as if he planned to take her elbow, but then he thought better of it and, without another word, he turned and walked away from her.

In the moonlit silence Jo watched him disappear and she wondered how on earth she could face the New Year without him.


Jo's mum telephoned several nights later. 'So how's it all going, love?'

'Terrific.' Jo gulped back the homesick tears that threatened the instant she heard her mum's voice. 'I've been having a really good time.'

'You don't sound too happy.'

'Must be a bad line. I'm fine, Mum. And Ivy's fine. How are you and everyone at home?'

'Oh, we're all chugging along the same as always. Not much news. Eric broke his arm. Silly kid jumped out of a tree, trying to frighten Grace.'

'Heavens. Poor Eric. I hope he's not in too much pain.'

'He'll live.'

'Give him my love. Give everyone my love.'

'I will. So…what have you been up to, Jo?'

'Well… I think everything's just about organised for Ivy.'

'Organised? How do you mean?'

Being organised and efficient was the way Jo had survived the past week. Luckily, it was how Hugh had chosen to conduct himself as well. They'd both been super-organised, mega-efficient and they'd deflected any superfluous emotion to Ivy.

'Hugh's had Ivy checked out by Simon Hallows, a fantastic burns specialist, who went to school with Hugh. You should have seen how gentle and kind he was with Ivy, Mum. And he's been able to set Hugh's mind at rest about what can be done for her in terms of future surgery as she grows.'

'The poor little lamb. She shouldn't have to go through all that.'

On the other end of the line there was the sound of a chair scraping and Jo could picture her mother sitting down, settling in for a comfortable chat. 'So you went along to the doctor's with them, did you?' Margie asked.

'Yes, Hugh wanted me there.'

'That's nice, love.'

The sentimental warmth in her mum's voice made Jo nervous. She'd done her best to squash Margie's wistful yearning for a romance between her daughter and the handsome English gentleman. She'd told her about Hugh's money and his aristocratic family and about Priscilla and the havoc she'd caused.

What else did it take to get the message across?

'We've found Ivy a school,' she said, hoping to steer the conversation away from uncomfortable topics. 'We've spent three days going to inspections at all the schools Hugh's friends have recommended, and he's found a lovely one only a few streets away from his house.'

'Sounds perfect. Does Ivy like it?'

'Loves it. Can't wait to start. You should have seen her face when she saw the little English schoolkids in their uniforms. The girls wear little green blazers and pleated skirts and knee-high socks. And the boys wear the cutest little green peaked caps. I think Ivy wanted to bring one of the boys home to keep him as a pet.'

Deep chuckles sounded on the other end of the line.

'And this afternoon we finished the interviews for a new nanny,' Jo added quickly.

'Oh?' There was no doubting the sudden tension in Margie's voice.

'It was such a hard choice. There were lots of very suitable girls, but I think Ivy will get on really well with the one we've settled on.'

'So you really are coming home?' Margie made no attempt to hide her disappointment.

'Of course I am. My holiday's almost over and I have to get back to work. I've already told you I'm flying out on Saturday.'

'I thought Hugh might have persuaded you to stay.'

'Well, he hasn't,' Jo said sharply, too sharply, but

it couldn't be helped. This wasn't her favourite talking point.

'Has he tried?' Margie asked.

'No.'

'I don't believe you.'

Oh, heck. There was nothing for it but to bite the bullet. 'Well, yes, he tried to talk me into staying— and not just as Ivy's nanny. But it wouldn't work, Mum.'

'Jo!'

'It wouldn't! Hugh came to his senses and realised his mistake.'

Jo was aware of a movement behind her and she turned to see Hugh in the doorway. She felt a rush of panic—her chest squeezed tight and her face felt as if she'd been sunburned. How long had he been there?

He'd taken up a casual pose, with his hands thrust deeply in his trouser pockets, his shoulder propped against the doorjamb and one foot crossed over the other.

The expression on his face was anything but casual.

Oh, God.

'Are you sure he wants you to go home, love?'

She could hardly hear her mum's voice above the pounding in her ears. Snatching her gaze from Hugh's, she twisted the phone cord with frantic fingers. 'Y-yes,' she said.

It was true. Hugh hadn't once this week tried to

convince her to stay. He'd never mentioned the engagement ring or his feelings. He'd been the perfect
courteous, polite English gentleman.

Until now. It wasn't very gentlemanly to listen in
on someone else's telephone conversation. The way
he watched her was downright intimidating.

There was a deep, loud sigh on the other end of
the line.

'We mustn't talk for too long now, Mum,' Jo said,
glancing again briefly in Hugh's direction. 'This call
must be costing you a fortune.'

'Before I forget, can you thank Hugh for the lovely
letter he sent?'

Again Jo's eyes flew to Hugh and he regarded her
with a dark, brooding vigilance that sent her heart-
strings twanging. She turned her back on him. 'What
did you say? Something about a letter?'

'Yes. Hugh sent us the loveliest long letter. He
must have written it last week, but it's only just arrived.'

'That—that's nice. OK, I'll thank him.'

Her mother gushed on. 'It was beautifully handwritten and he thanked us for sharing Christmas dinner with him. Said he'd never enjoyed a Christmas
more. And he invited us all to England.'

'You're joking.'

'No, seriously. He thought we'd love his family's
farm in Devon. And he went to the trouble of telling
each one of us specific things we'd enjoy.'

'What—what kind of specific things?'

'Well…let me see…' There was a crackle of paper. 'He said Brad and Nick should try polo because they're such good horsemen…and Bill and Eric could go exploring on the moors…and Tilly and Grace would love the little Dartmoor ponies. And if we go in the spring there'd be wild flowers and market villages that I'd love and he has a good trout fishing stream for your dad.'

Jo sent a quick, frantic glance back over her shoulder to the doorway. Hugh had gone again, leaving as silently as he'd appeared. She ought to feel relieved, but she felt strangely bereft. She forced her mind back to the conversation. 'Hugh didn't actually name everyone in the family individually, did he?'

'Yes, he did, love. He remembered the names of everyone. I thought he must have checked them with you.'

*No, no he didn't.*

'Wasn't that nice of him?' her mum added.

'Very.'

Jo couldn't believe it. None of her friends in Brisbane had ever been able to remember the names of all her brothers and sisters—not even her flatmates—and she'd been living with them for four years and they'd even visited Bindi Creek with her.

*She'd known Hugh for two weeks.* He'd spent one day with her family. One day and he could remember them all—Nick, Brad, Bill, Eric, Grace and Tilly.

OK, so he had an excellent memory for names. There was no need to get all choked up about a man's memory. 'Well, I'm sorry you won't be coming over here now,' she said.

'Yeah,' Margie sighed.

'Mum, I'm looking forward to seeing you all very soon.'

There was silence from the other end of the line.

'Mum, are you there? I should say goodbye now.'

'All right. Goodbye, love.'

'I'll see you really soon.'

'Yes, have a safe trip.' Her mum sounded so dejected as she rang off that Jo burst into tears.

# CHAPTER TEN

'NO AIRPORT farewells,' Jo insisted. 'It would be too traumatic for Ivy.'

Somewhat reluctantly, Hugh agreed.

And so the goodbyes took place at St Leonard's Terrace.

He watched the shining dampness in Jo's eyes as she hugged Ivy for the last time. He watched her tight white face as she held out her hand to shake his. He watched her back—ramrod straight—as she walked to the car behind Humphries.

And he saw that she didn't look back and she didn't wave once, not even as the car turned the corner.

The plan was that Humphries would drive her to Heathrow while Hugh stayed behind to keep Ivy entertained with the wind-up pink pig he'd ordered from the toy department in Harrods.

But how in hell's name was a man supposed to entertain a child when his heart was breaking? Especially when the child persisted in asking awkward questions about when Jo was coming back, or why there had to be a new nanny.

'I don't want a new nanny. I want Jo,' she repeated over and over as they sat on the floor in her bedroom and made a poor attempt to play with the toy that had so delighted her a week ago.

'You'll like Sally, your new nanny,' Hugh said, wishing he could dredge up an enthusiasm he couldn't feel.

Ivy's lower lip pouted ominously. 'But I love Jo.'

'Jo explained it to you, poppet. She has to go home to Australia. Now, look at this lovely fat pig. Isn't he funny? He's walking right under your bed. I think we need to get Howard to—'

'I don't want Jo to go to Australia,' Ivy said, pushing the treasured toy away. 'I want her here.'

'Well, aren't you a Miss Bossy Boots?' Hugh wondered how he would cope if his daughter threw a tantrum.

'Why did you let her go, Daddy?'

He wasn't ready for that question. 'I don't know,' he whispered hoarsely.

Ivy stared up at him with curious green eyes. 'Daddy, are you crying?'

'No.'

'You are.'

'No, no.' He blinked hard. 'It's just something in my eye.'

Scrambling to her feet, Ivy looked worried. She pushed her little face close up to his till their noses were almost touching and she stared anxiously into his eyes. 'You *are* sad,' she said. 'You're very sad.'

'Just a little.'

'Is it because Jo had to go away? Doesn't she love us?'

'I'm sure she loves us, poppet, but she loves her family too.'

'Does she love Tilly and Grace better'n us?'

Hugh forced a smile and he hugged Ivy close. 'She couldn't possibly love anyone more than she loves us.'

'Don't worry, Daddy. She'll come back.'

'No, poppet, you've got to understand Jo's not coming back.'

Ivy's eyes were huge. 'She's gone for good?'

'Yes.' Hugh sighed.

From her lonely seat in the back of the car, Jo watched the streets of London flash past. This was her last glimpse of the famous city. There would be no more chances to visit London's wonderful museums or art galleries, or to go to lovely concerts like the one Anne Eliot had taken her to in St Martin-in-the-Fields.

Never again would she take Ivy for walks along the Thames Embankment, or go to the King's Road to buy sweets from the little shop around the corner.

Worst of all—very, *very* worst of all—there were no more chances to see Hugh and Ivy.

She'd come to the end. The final page. And she'd discovered what she'd suspected all along; her story was a gritty reality drama, not a fairy tale.

She'd accused Hugh of creating a fairy tale but, if

that were so, he would have found a way to stop her from leaving. He would have done the Hollywood thing—chased after her and swept her into his arms and vowed his undying love for her. Or he would have found a magical fairy tale way to *prove* beyond doubt that he loved her.

Instead he'd shaken her by the hand.

And he'd said goodbye with a strange little stiff nod of his head. How jolly British!

How bloody awful! Her face crumpled and her tears overflowed and streamed down her cheeks. And her chest hurt with the awful pain of wanting Hugh. It was her fault that she'd lost him. She'd walked away from him. But she loved him! Oh, dear heaven, she loved him so much.

She loved looking at him, she loved talking to him, she loved being with him and she loved making plans for Ivy with him. She loved his friends, his parents, living in his house, his city…

There wasn't a thing about Hugh Strickland that she didn't love.

Another torrent of tears poured down her face and she reached into her pocket for a tissue to stem the flow. Along with the tissue, a stiff piece of paper came out of her pocket and, as she mopped her face, she stared at it lying in her lap.

Actually…it wasn't a sheet of paper; it was an envelope—with a single word written in spiky black handwriting.

*Jo.*

It was Hugh's handwriting.

Her heartbeats seemed to stop and then they began a querulous thumping. She turned the envelope over and slipped her little finger beneath the flap. *What on earth could it be?*

Inside, there was a single sheet of notepaper and something else. Something small. Her eyes caught a glint of gold and her hand trembled as she reached inside.

A ring! Oh, dear Lord. Hugh's grandmother's engagement ring. Her heart picked up pace until it thundered. Her hands shook so badly she almost dropped the ring, so she slipped it on to her finger for safekeeping and opened the piece of paper to read a handwritten message.

*Dearest Jo,*

*I am desperately in love with you. I know it's hard for you to believe; it's all happened so quickly—how can I convince you?*

*I feel as if my past has happened in another lifetime, and all I know now is that with you by my side I could live my life as it's meant to be. If you were my wife I would be the happiest man in all history and I would devote my days to making you happy too.*

*If ever or whenever you decide that you want me, all you need to do is slip this ring on your finger and come back to me and I'll be yours for ever.*

*If you return the ring I'll know that I've been wrong in thinking you love me too.*

*I love you.*

*Hugh*

'Pigs don't usually go in the same pen as unicorns,' Hugh patiently explained to Ivy.

His daughter frowned at him. 'Why not?' She didn't like being corrected.

'They eat different things.'

'Unicorns eat grass. What do pigs eat?'

'Oh, grain and scraps—almost anything really.'

An impish grin suffused Ivy's face. 'Like you.'

'Are you calling me a pig?'

She giggled. 'Yes, you're a pig, Daddy. You eat almost anything.'

'I beg your pardon. I don't think I can let you get away with that. Little girls who call their fathers pigs must be tickled.'

'No.'

'I'm going to have to tickle you to death.'

'No!' Ivy shouted again, but she was giggling too and her fate was sealed.

Toys scattered as the two of them tumbled sideways on the carpet. Next minute Hugh was on his back holding Ivy up in the air at arm's length and the little girl was laughing and squealing.

'Is this a private party or can anyone join in?'

Hugh paused in mid-tickle. His heart jolted hard. Had he heard what he thought he'd heard?

He turned.

And there was Jo standing at the top of the stairs, just outside the doorway to Ivy's room.

Her face, framed by her neat brown hair, looked pale and yet bright spots of colour stood out in her cheeks. She sent them a rather wobbly smile.

'Jo!' Ivy screamed. 'It's Jo, Daddy! I told you she'd come back!'

As soon as Hugh lowered her to the floor Ivy dashed across the room to fling herself at Jo, and Hugh's heart pounded so fiercely he felt it might burst through the wall of his chest.

Jo was back.

Jo, smiling across at him as she hugged Ivy. Jo, with raindrops in her hair and with sparkling, lovely eyes—looking as if she might cry.

Hugh swallowed the painful lump in his throat.

Silver tears glistened on her lashes as she looked at him. 'You remembered all their names,' she said.

'I did?' He had no idea what she was talking about, but he pushed himself to his feet.

'My family. My brothers and sisters—you remembered their names.'

'That's why you came back?'

'It was so sweet of you to remember, Hugh.'

She wasn't making sense. Hugh felt his elation falter.

But then Jo held out her hand—her left hand—and he saw the twinkle of rubies and diamonds.

He wasn't sure who moved first, or how they came together. All he knew was that he was holding Jo at last. He was clasping her tight, breathing in the special fragrance of her, feeling her arms around him and her sweet body pressing close, and she was welcoming him with open lips, kissing him, wanting him.

'I love you, Hugh,' she whispered against his lips. 'I love you. I love you. I love you.' She kissed him on his mouth and on his chin, on the underside of his jaw, his throat and then his lips again.

Laughing, he caught her eager face between his hands and held her still so that he could return her kisses, so that he could kiss her soft, warm mouth and her salty tears. And then he hugged her to him, almost afraid that she might disappear.

'Daddy! Stop it, you're squeezing Jo too hard!' Impatient little hands tugged at their clothing.

Breathless, they broke apart and looked down at Ivy as if she'd just arrived from outer space.

'Ah, poppet,' said Hugh. 'Why don't you run down to the kitchen and see if Regina has afternoon tea ready for you?'

'Has she made chocolate cake?'

'Perhaps. Why don't you go and ask her?'

'OK. See you.' At the top of the stairs, Ivy turned back and she eyed them warily. 'Make sure Jo doesn't go away again.'

'Don't worry, Ivy, I promise I'm here to stay,' Jo assured her.

His daughter set off happily downstairs and Hugh took Jo's hands in his and looked again at the ring. It suited her hand beautifully. 'I've been so worried,' he said. 'I didn't know if you would find this, or when you'd find it, or how you'd react, or what you'd do, or whether—'

Jo stopped him by placing two fingers against his lips. 'It's OK, Hugh. I'm here.'

And then they were lost in another kiss—an unrestrained, lush and lingering kiss—a kiss that released at last all the loving and longing that had lain in their hearts.

It was much, much later that Jo told him her story. 'We were on the approach into Heathrow. You know where all those big hotels are. Poor Humphries didn't know what to make of me when I started blubbering that we had to turn around. He was so worried I'd miss my plane. It took me ages to convince him that I *wanted* to miss it. Once he realised I was serious he broke the speed limit to get me back here.' She blushed sweetly. 'To you.'

Just for that Hugh kissed her again. 'You do understand that I truly love you, don't you?'

'Yes, Hugh.' She lifted a hand to gently caress his cheek. 'Yes.'

'I'm the luckiest man alive.'

She dropped her head on to his shoulder and Hugh pressed kisses to the back of her neck. 'I know I've been far too rushed about this, but when can we be married? Is six months too soon?'

'Oh, goodness, six months?' Her eyes danced with silent laughter. 'I couldn't possibly wait that long.'

# EPILOGUE

*One of the best kept secrets on the London social calendar last week was the sudden and very private wedding of Lord Strickland, long-time Chelsea bachelor and owner of Rychester Aviation.*

*Always first with the spiciest news, this column blew the lid off Hugh Strickland's clandestine romance with Australian nanny, Jo Berry.*

*We made startling revelations and saucy suggestions about what would happen to the unfortunate miss from Down Under.*

*Humble pie is not usually on the menu in this column. However, dear readers, I will eat a large slice since my predictions about this couple fell so wide of the mark.*

*Who would have guessed that True Love would play an unexpected hand, and that Miss Bindi Creek would become Lady Joanna Strickland, wife of the future Earl of Rychester?*

*This columnist was somehow overlooked by the minions who prepared the guest list for the Strickland-Berry wedding, as were most others* apart from family and a few close friends, who gathered at the chapel on the Rychester estate in Devon.

However, I can report that the bride looked radiant, the bridesmaid very sweet, and that the post-wedding celebrations continued for several days.

I am reliably informed that Jo Berry's extended family from Australia were flown over on one of Strickland's private jets. No small order considering there are enough Berrys to field a cricket team.

My spies tell me that the honeymooners—with a little companion—have been seen in the French Alps, in New York and in Tahiti...and I have no reason to doubt any of them.

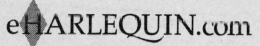

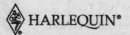
# Coming Next Month

### #3875 HER SPANISH BOSS Barbara McMahon
*9 to 5*

When Rachel Goodson starts working for Luis Alvares, he's prickly and suspicious. But soon they draw closer and secrets spill out. Luis's heart is still with his late wife, so Rachel is stunned when he wants her to pose as his girlfriend. Then Luis makes it clear he wants more than just a pretend relationship….

### #3876 IN THE ARMS OF THE SHEIKH Sophie Weston

Natasha Lambert is horrified by what she must wear as her best friend's bridesmaid! Worse, the best man is Kazim al Saraq—an infuriatingly charming sheikh with a dazzling wit and an old-fashioned take on romance. He's determined to win Natasha's heart—and Natasha is terrified he might succeed…!

### #3877 A BRIDE WORTH WAITING FOR Caroline Anderson
*Heart to Heart*

Annie Shaw believes her boyfriend, Michael Harding, died in a brutal attack nine years ago. Little does she know that he has been forced to live undercover. Now Michael is free to pick up his life and reveal himself to the woman he loves. Can Annie fall in love with the man he has become?

### #3878 A FAMILY TO BELONG TO Natasha Oakley

Once, Kate loved Gideon from afar—but he was married and had the kind of family life Kate knew she could never have. Now, years later, Kate meets Gideon again—bringing up his children alone. They long to get close—but that will mean finding the courage to confront the past…and find a future.